A Guide
To Deduction
2nd Edition

Hannah Rogers

Paperback ISBN 978-1-78705-239-0
ePub ISBN 978-1-78705-240-6
PDF ISBN 978-1-78705-241-3

Published in the UK by MX Publishing
335 Princess Park Manor, Royal Drive, London, N11 3GX
www.mxpublishing.co.uk

Cover design by Brian Belanger

1

For more deductions and Sherlock Holmes content daily, visit:
http://aguidetodeduction.tumblr.com/

Dedicated to:
The Sherlock Holmes in my blood, from my grandfather, Colin.
The love of writing encouraged by my grandfather, John.
The theories and thoughts shared with friends, particularly Ciara, Tilda, Cemre, Camilla, Hazel and Zahrah.
And you, dedicated readers, for forcing me to get my head in gear and finish this thing.

Contents

4

An Introduction to Deduction

'You see, but you do not observe. The distinction is clear.'

                - Sherlock Holmes, A Scandal in Bohemia

The work of detective is considered glamourous and romantic by many people, my own companion Watson included. However, this façade is little more than smoke and mirrors. Deduction, or induction as some call it, is reliant upon nothing more than observation. Connections which appear to be the product of clairvoyance or magic are made entirely tangible.

This book exists to make those threads of logic between seemingly unconnected details clear. To tell a man's profession by his thumb, one must first know what know to look for the thumb. There are infinite invisible threads of logic around us. All it takes it to know what threads to unpick, and what one's to tie together.

Best of luck,

                Sherlock Holmes

Tips

1. An in-depth knowledge of human anatomy is vital. This includes the body both before and after death.

2. Once you eliminate the impossible, whatever remains, no matter how improbable, must be the truth.

3. Gender means very little in the area of deduction: women and men are quite evenly matched in ability despite differing physical builds. Individuals who defies a stereotype is the fastest way to throw off such assumptions.

4. Observation is the first step to deduction. Focus on the cuffs, sleeve, knees and elbows, as this is the clothing which comes into contact with the most surfaces.

5. It is important to note when inferring from dialect how a person learned the language and whether the teacher was native speaker. People who learn in class have a better grasp of technicalities yet self-taught people often have trouble with grammar.

6. If someone, in sharing a deduction, includes very specific conditions about a person, the more likely it is that the person submitting it demonstrates those aspects themselves.

7. When looking for the perpetrator of a crime, motive is the essential element.

8. Despite what the internet may tell you, there is no reliable way to discern the gender or age of a person online without honest confirmation.

9. Women have 14-16 parts of their brain dedicated to communication which includes body language etc. whereas men only have 4-6. This means that women are often perceived to have better communication ability.

Work

"Being a consultant has the benefit of freedom from the demon of consistent work. Boredom, though a bitter side effect, proves to exceed the drag of employment. Skills and ability can often be derived from work, though hard labour tends to scratch the sheen off a skill. Heaven forbid it should ever happen to a mind like mine. Work may be a motivator, but is often a motive to much darker things."

SH

10. Long clean fingernails are a sign that the person does little manual work. Dirty and short fingernails are a sign of manual labour.

11. If someone has well-tended hands with no callouses and healthy long nails, but dirtied and rough skin, it suggests they have been working in manual labour for a short time.

12. Long or fake nails on both hands can also indicate that the person wearing them is unlikely to currently work in a medical field, such as a veterinarian, doctor or nurse; they are uncomfortable for patients and can be obstructing.

13. Many teachers who work in less technologically advanced school have marks of chalk on their fingernails or clothing.

14. Someone who has worked in theatre tech for a while will often respond "thank you" when given directions or told a "plan of action," if distracted. (For example, "I'm going out." "Thank you.")

15. A singer is more likely to breathe from his or her diaphragm. You can tell because when they take a deep breath, rather than their chest rising or falling, they seem to suck in their gut.

16. Opera singers tend to have broad shoulders as the muscles around their diaphragm build, leading to the cliché of the "fat lady".

17. If someone is an opera singer, he tends to talk in a higher register so as not to damage the voice.

18. Opera singers tend to have a straight spine as part of their posture and keep their head "loose."

19. A trained singer's shoulders will not move up and down when he breathes as it both lets the least amount of air in and looks unprofessional.

20. A trained vocalist will often speak with a more resonant sound, since he has been trained to let sound vibrate through the mask of his face.

21. When someone is signing and he doesn't open his mouth wide when pronouncing vocals, it is possible that he has experience in a chorus.

22. An experienced actor may breathe from his diaphragm to improve their voice projection.

23. Actors/performers may also be inclined to stand at "neutral": feet shoulder-width apart, knees very slightly bent, shoulders back, abdominal muscles relaxed.

24. Actors may get into the habit of speaking in a higher volume and level of elocution.

25. Small rectangular patches on the back of the neck may be where microphone tape has ripped off the hairs.

26. Someone who served in the military may show many signs of communal living, as most daily routines are shared, such as meals.

27. Training nurses or medical assistants often walk around in practical, quality shoes.

28. Training nurses or medical assistants are often overly conscious of their health choices.

29. Training nurses or medical assistants rarely wear makeup and tie their hair up frequently.

30. Hairdressers will often have a callus on the outside of their top knuckle on the ring finger of their dominant hand, due to the way they hold their equipment.

31. If a person is a hairdresser, he is likely to get cuts on the middle finger of his non-dominant hand.

32. (See above) Rounded crescent cuts pointing upwards belong to rounded tipped scissors commonly used by barbers.

33. (See above) Sharper straight cuts indicate the use of hairdresser's scissors.

34. An artist who has very short fingernails is more likely to be a sculptor as long nails can break/cause pain to the artist while working on the pottery wheel because of the pressure used against the clay with one's hands to manipulate it into shape.

35. A person working in the architecture industry has a tendency to observe building elements above anything. (For example, windows and structure of walls.)

36. A chef or someone working in food might have irregular cuts and burns on their hands and arms, but otherwise have very clean hands with short nails.

37. If a person has artificial nails or natural nails longer than one-quarter inch, they are not any form of hospital staff: long nails spread infections and are not allowed in clinical settings.

38. Someone who has worked in hospitality will often stay "behind" when walking behind someone or trying to get past a person, rather than "excuse me" etc.

39. People who work in small quarters may use simple one word commands like "behind" when trying to get past a person.

40. People who work using their hands usually sneeze into the crook of their elbow on impulse, even when they have tissues on hand. (Like those who handle food, chemicals, lab equipment.)

41. Someone working in a bakery will have several little cuts all over his hands, due to the crust of hot bread: they will also have flour on their shoes.

42. Someone who needs to present as part of his job will frequently check how he looks, possibly carrying a mirror with him at all times

43. Someone who needs to present as part of his job will also most likely talk "with his hands" to emphasise points.

44. Black, green and red are the most common white board pen colours, and having any combination of these inks smeared on the fingertips or side of the hand suggests that a person works with a whiteboard, most commonly teachers.

45. The same traces of colour on the lips or tongue suggest they use a projector and water soluble markers.

46. These inks stain very badly on fabric, and are often possible to find even after the material has been washed.

47. Police officers will have an unusual walk. This is due to the massive amount of equipment they typically have to carry on their belts.

48. If a person is unusually quick with knowing the alphabetical order of letters, chances are they work at/frequently use a library.

49. You can tell if someone is a digital artist, or at least not used to working in traditional media, if they have a noticeable callous on the outer palm heel of their dominant hand.

50. If someone works in both traditional and digital mediums, they will lack this callous: due to trying to avoid smudging their work.

51. You can often tell a supermarket cashier from the bruises and scrapes around their hands and wrists often caused by swift, and sometimes clumsy, handling of a range of items and materials.

52. Someone who works in a coffee shop will have outer clothes that smell of coffee while his everyday clothes will not. This is because most coffee shops require a uniform, but people don't get new coats for an indoor job, so the coat will be hung up in the back, absorbing the smell. Soft fabrics are more prone to this.

53. If someone works at a desk often, they are unlikely to wear bracelets or a watch as clattering against the surface of the desk can get annoying.

54. Most militaries don't allow long hair or not being clean shaven, so people who work in the military tend to maintain these appearances even during time off from work.

55. A small but pronounced callous on the large knuckle of the right index finger often indicates someone who works in retail: built in card-swipers are most commonly on the right hand side of the till, and the action of swiping cards repeatedly rubs at the knuckle.

14

56. If someone wears a lot of jewellery but none on his dominant hand, it may mean he is an artist who wants to make sure his jewellery doesn't get in the way or dirty.

57. If a young civilian often stands with feet shoulder width apart and his hands behind his back, he most likely took part in a military-based class in school such JROTC or spent a lot of time in detention centres as a juvenile.

58. To figure out which one, observe how they walk. A former JROTC cadet will naturally adjust his or her footsteps to be in cadence with your own, while someone who spent time in detention centres will not.

59. Actors and dancers often automatically stand with their hands behind their back since it allows them to maximise their breathing.

60. People who know shorthand typically work in careers which require a quick relaying of information, such as a typist in court or a journalist.

61. People with irregular scratches on their arms and hands may work with animals, due to the conflicting angles, size and depth of scratches.

62. Sometimes car salesman wear their belt buckles to the side so that when they lean up against the cars there is no risk of scratching the paint.

63. Actors are often more likely to be smokers, due to the indefinite periods of waiting between rehearsals/filming/scenes, leaving them few options to fill the time that can end as soon as they are needed.

64. However, dancers and singers are less likely to smoke in these gaps, due to their critical need of high lung capacity. (Note the occasional use as a weight suppressant and addictive nature.)

65. If an artist has stains and holes in his clothes from chemicals it is likely he has been using tougher materials, such as print making which requires chemicals to eat away at steel to create a pattern. The holes will be more severe than basic cleaning supplies, which are far weaker.

66. Surgeons commonly have small indentations on their forefingers from cutting open and sewing up a patient: if these marks are very pronounced they were in surgery very recently.

67. You can tell an artist by the way he holds the utensil, with the last digit of his forefinger

completely against it: this gives them more control of the movement of the line.

68. When retrieving something from a lower shelf, a person who will squat on his haunches rather than bending over it is likely either to have worked at or frequently used a library, bookstore or convenience store.

69. If a person walks around all day with his shirt on backwards or similar, it may indicate he is in a position of authority (no one wanted to embarrass them) but not a public figure (no-one needed to tell them about it).

70. If someone has long, thin callouses along the back of their heel, it could be an indication of wearing boots frequently, particularly industrial/work boots.

Questions for Sherlock

Q: *What do you do other than detective work?*
A: I enjoy the study of bees: they are fascinating to me. Dangerous when threatened, hierarchical, and complex.
Watson once called them "miniature humans".
He may have been right.
SH

Q: *What's the best way to learn a lot about a new roommate?*
A: Drag them to crime scenes against their will, or develop your deductive prowess to the point where one glance tells you all you need.
Do both, if necessary.
SH

Q: *How can you fake confidence?*
A: Eye contact that cannot be broken with a sledgehammer.
Wit sharp enough to cleave diamonds.
Love yourself enough to make anyone around you a moon orbiting the planet of your ego.
SH

Q: *What do you do if someone strangles you?*

A: Try not to die.
SH

Q: *What's your favourite book?*
A: Practical Handbook of Bee Culture, with some Observations upon the Segregation of the Queen.
SH

Q: *Are there any tools an aspiring Consulting Detective should own and always carry with them?*
A: A John Watson, or equivalent.
SH

Q: *What is the correct way to disarm someone?*
A: Carefully.
SH

Q: *Do you often find yourself analysing others when you'd rather not?*
A: It is always good to analyse others.
It is not always good to let them know this.
SH

Q: *Any advice for someone hoping to follow in your footsteps?*
A: Don't.
SH

Q: *How often do you actually use John Watson's medical knowledge? Surely you remember enough about it to work without him.*

A: I am not an expert in all things.

John holds knowledge of human biology: something necessary when investigating how it has failed catastrophically.

You cannot investigate a murder without first understanding it.

SH

Q: *Have you ever come across a case that you had little or no expertise in?*

A: Frequently, so I become an expert.

Research is 90 per cent of my job, however much chronicles of my work would like to persuade you otherwise.

SH

Writing

The written word is still a major form of communication, despite its increasing outdated nature. To analyse someone's writing is to know them better as a person. It is a skill which is invaluable in detective work.

SH

71. People may write in tiny lettering when they want to save on paper or present as much information as possible: this can lead to uncharacteristic handwriting.

72. When writing under observation, such as in exam conditions, handwriting often becomes neater due to a subconscious need to impress.

73. A defined but hard to read signature is a sign that the person has to sign his name frequently, becoming lazy when writing the predetermined name.

74. A person who writes awkwardly or slowly is probably used to communicating through typed messages and storing information digitally rather than on paper.

75. You can tell the keys most used on a personal computer keyboard by looking at which ones are the most smooth; they have been worn down the most.

76. The more handwriting slants to the right, the faster the author was writing.

77. The easiest way to tell if a signature is a forgery is through absolutely precise lines, and darker point of ink; these are frequently signs of hesitation.

78. When writing the date, like 1/2/14, if the slashes are at two different angles it could mean that the person paused when determining the middle number.

79. When observing handwriting, if the person uses all capitals and is printing, he has likely been conditioned to writing in such a way from work that requires clear communication.

80. If someone's handwriting is slanted on a lined piece of paper, he was likely copying from another page, therefore not paying attention to his own paper.

Mind Palaces

Basic facts:

While it is now known as a Mind or Memory Palace, this form of thought originated as "the method of loci" in ancient Greece. Its aim was to capitalise on the idea that the mind is better at remembering locations than facts. A mind palace is the memorisation of a layout familiar to you which contains images, objects or concepts which trigger your memory though association. A mind palace is a memory aid, not a memory in and of itself. You have to be aware of storing things in there in order for them to be there when you use it. In other words, if you have not taken time to "store" your memory trigger, it will not be in your mind palace. This method is typically restricted to a small area to keep it easier to remember, such as a single room. This is where Sherlock's discussion of "limited space" comes from. When using a larger mind palace, it is sometimes useful to "mime" movement through it, though this is rarely necessary.

First steps

For your first attempt to be as successful as possible, remove all distractions possible: close your eyes and block out sound.

Prepare yourself as you would for meditation: both are disorientating but oddly refreshing.

Decide upon your "palace." Ironically, it's best to avoid large spaces you don't know well since they are difficult to maintain effectively. Instead choose a real place you know intimately, such as your bedroom.

Picture your "palace." At this point, all you require is the size and spacing of the room with bulkier furniture. Smaller details (such as books) will be added later. Familiarise yourself with everything by walking around.

Repeat this until you've a clear image in your mind which you can recall accurately with relative ease. It may take several days, but don't fret. It's a learning process; mastering your first palace is the hardest part.

Storing Things

You must take the same route through your palace each time; otherwise, you'll likely get a mental block. If you are searching for something in particular, you can abandon the palace as soon as you find what you want, but when you're storing information always travel through the same route. It just helps keep things more ordered.

The best triggers are either absolutely ridiculous or logical leaps.

An example of the logical leap: "I had to remember that 'Belief In' is an attitudinal belief, involving personal choices and values, while 'Belief That' is a factual belief."

"Our belief in Sherlock is a feeling and that feeling governs the fact; the fact that Sherlock isn't a fake informs our feelings of belief in him. So I have a badge on someone's lapel which has a silhouette of Sherlock with the phrase 'I Believe in Sherlock Holmes' across it.

That little badge means I can remember everything I need to about that hypothesis; about four pages of solid text in the book."

An example of the ridiculous trigger: "I had to remember quotations saying that Charles Dickens promoted left wing politics in a sarcastic way in "Oliver Twist," so I remember a bird with a corkscrew on its left wing."

"The bird's left wing illustrates the political nature, the corkscrew reminds both of the title "Twist" and 'screwed' nature of discussion. This unfortunate bird triggers several pages worth of supportive quotations."

Storing Things: Advanced

Interconnecting comes in when you want to remember more. An earlier example mentioned that the Sherlock badge was on someone's lapel; not only is that person a trigger himself, but their interactions with other objects set off other triggers. However, interconnecting like this isn't for everyone. You may find it easier placing things in succession, like on a shelf. This works just as well with simpler trains of though, though as your line of items gets longer, it may become confusing.

At the end of the day, the complexity of your palace is entirely your choice.

Overview

Getting mind palaces to work effectively for you is very difficult.

It is normal, perhaps even expected, for you to have to redesign and change your mind palace multiple times.

Mind palaces made quickly are best for temporary storage of things like shopping lists and phone numbers. If you plan on using a mind palace for long-term memory or use under stress, such as an exam, it's best to have everything in place at least a month before.

A long-term palace is a commitment as your mind's a bit like your muscles; if it's not used your palace will fade. You don't have to update it every day, just check in and review to ensure everything's where it's supposed to be.

Sport

My interest in sport is limited to purely those of self-defence, and yet any sport can be influential in a situation such as this. Do they know how to throw a punch? Does their sport help them take one? In more mundane scenarios it may help to stimulate conversation or some other facade of normality. I fail to see how this can be considered essential information, other than when under the guise of a fake identity.

SH

81. Clean/new shoes with worn down soles are used for regular running, probably inside.

82. Walking speed is proportional to pressure placed on the toe and thus can be observed through a footprint.

83. A slow gait will have a greater indentation at the back, a lighter one at the front.

84. A runner's footprint will have a minor or non-existent heel print.

85. An avid jogger usually has a more pronounced "roll" in his feet (when taking a step forward, first planting his heel and then the foot "rolls" forward

until only the toes touch the pavement) than people who don't jog.

86. People who have been running for a long time typically have strong muscle definition on their legs.

87. A golfer will often have one hand less tanned than the other due to the glove that they wear.

88. There are a few ways you can tell if someone has had martial arts training in the past: 1. If you can see them walk around barefoot they will walk more on the blades (outsides) of their feet.

89. 2. How they move their hands when talking. Martial artists have thumbs slightly tucked in toward the palm, the fingers are never really straight, and they will have a slight bend in the middle knuckles.

90. 3. Depending on how dedicated they were, the outside/ridge of their hands and their proximal phalanges (knuckles) on their index and middle finger could be slightly calloused from repetitive striking of objects.

91. People who have been trained to fight will clench their fists with thumbs on the outside to avoid breaking their thumbs if they throw a punch.

92. In a standoff situation, a martial artist will most likely step back with his right foot and turn it so it

points slightly outward, shifting his weight to the back foot.

93. By comparison, someone not trained will probably spread their feet apart, and centre themselves.

94. A person who danced as a child, especially in ballet, will stand and walk with feet pointing slightly outwards as an adult.

95. It is rare for a ballet dancer to have bad posture.

96. Dancers typically have above average memorisation skills due to the nature of their career.

97. If a female's feet are covered in callouses and blisters, primarily on the toes and edges of her feet, she could be a pointe dancer.

98. A) The more callouses = the longer they've been dancing

99. B) The more blisters = the less experienced, but practicing often.

100. C) Pointe dancers often have short flat (but not rounded) toe nails.

101. People who have danced ballet may hold their hand with their middle finger slightly bent.

102. Dancers may have a tendency to walk toe-heel, particularly when in a hurry.

103. The main difference between ballerinas and gymnasts would be the upper body: Ballerinas do not need such great arm and shoulder strength.

104. If a person when falling automatically does a roll fall (a forward roll to protect them from falling), it indicates they may practise karate, parkour or other "extreme" sports regularly.

105. People who react to stress or fear by tensing their back muscles or shifting subtly to a defensive stance tend to have studied martial arts in the past.

106. An avid fencer will often have visibly uneven muscle tone in his legs.

107. A fencer may move his feet into an L-shaped position if he is put into a tense, stressful or scary situation, and may raise his dominant hand slightly, so that his pose resembles an "en garde" position.

108. If a person first starts with his left hand to shake a person's hand, he is probably a right-handed fencer and is used to doing most handshakes with his left hand.

109. A person who is experienced in horse riding will grip straps in the same way reins are held. This can

also tell if they are an English or Western rider, as the way the strap is held differs.

110. People who practice yoga have a definitive way of breathing to centre their energy; they will breathe slowly on counts of three, filling first their diaphragm, then their ribcage, then their chest.

111. If someone has a cauliflower ear, you can reasonably deduce that he participates in some kind of contact sport, such as wrestling, rugby or martial arts.

112. A person with callouses on the first joint of his three middle fingers on one hand is likely to have practised archery for a significant amount of time. These callouses develop due to contact with the bow string, they appear after around a month of regular practise but can last a long time.

113. Many devout rowers will have callouses on both hands, usually on their palms, near where the fingers meet the palm.

114. A series of shallow, broad scabs or scars along a small area is indicative of an active sport player who scrapes themselves the same way frequently: in the case of the interiors of elbows, often volleyball players.

115. People who walk toe-heel may also perform street acrobatics as they train to walk like this so as not to ruin their knees while running over concrete.

116. You can tell someone has had martial arts training when you shake his hand. Their index finger will extend out when clasping the hand of another. It's thought as a way to prevent the other person from attacking you.

117. A main difference between gymnasts and dancers is that gymnasts will arch their backs while dancers try to keep their back completely straight.

118. If someone is wearing sneakers with abrasions near the front outside, this indicates that they are a skateboarder or have skateboarded in the past.

119. If the sole of only one shoe is worn out and cracked it would be reasonable to assume that the wearer skateboards, due to the force of hitting the pavement to propel the board would wear it down.

120. A good indicator of someone who longboards will be that he prefers shoes that have thinner soles. These make it easier to feel the board and adjust balance accordingly.

121. Long boarders tend to use their board to get around and go longer distances. Meanwhile, skateboarders typically use their boards for tricks.

122. An athlete who does sports relying on upper body strength will often end up with knots in his shoulders and neck.

123. People trained in figure skating will often stand and sit with arched backs.

124. Unlike other dancers, figure skaters' sense of balance and normal coordination off of the ice may be terrible.

125. Trained ice skaters are particularly good at falling down unharmed due to the fact they were most likely taught proper falling technique.

126. Untrained skaters may suffer from a bruised tail bone due to the basic instinct to fall on the back rather than the head.

127. Skateboarders wear down their shoes at the toe and heel due to nature of ollies (or jumps) performed on the board.

128. Callouses at the base of the pinkie and ring finger on the dominant hand could be a result of playing sports like tennis and baseball.

129. Most swimmers will have tiny speckled bruises on only one shin due to getting in and out of the pool and using their shin for support.

130. Dancers are often highly aware of their alignment and posture, often walking with their feet perfectly parallel.

131. Rock climbers can be identified by their calloused hands, short fingernails, large forearms and rounded shoulders.

132. Many rock climbers have slightly misshapen feet due to tight climbing shoes.

133. A roller skater attempting to ice skate will often damage his ankles due to the different centre of balance.

134. When gymnasts hold something, such as a steering wheel, they generally do not wrap their thumbs around, and instead keep their thumbs next to their index fingers. This habit comes from practicing on the uneven bars.

135. Dancers, gymnasts and athletes tend not have any "bangs" or fringes because they would be distracting if not pinned up properly.

136. Martial artists have been known to move around on the ball of their foot more than average out of combat scenarios.

137. With most dedicated ballet dancer's feet, their big toes tend to curve towards the rest of their toes due to the constrictive nature of their shoes.

138. Soccer players will have a tan line right below their knee from shin guards.

Self Defence

This section is written in regard to a dozen different forms of combat I have learned over the years. To engage in combat is something best avoided, regardless of situation. However, there is often a need to defend oneself from someone less courteous. This is to be considered a starting point, nothing more.

SH

Attacking with hands:

In a close quarters situation, there are only a few body parts you can rely on to make a strong attack. The hand is a reliable one, but predictable. Be aware your opponent will expect you to attack using your hands. The sting of a slap may catch him more off guard than a punch. Also be aware that you should wrap your thumb around the outside of your fist instead of inside: having your thumb inside your fist can lead to breaking it. Avoid punching any dense areas: hitting the jaw may be effective but it can break your hand. (This is why people wear boxing gloves.) Also consider using the heel of your palm, as a tough and easy to manoeuvre attack. Pressing against the nose with the heel of a palm can break the nose with relative ease.

Attacking with feet:

A kick is rarely effective in an instance of hand-to-hand combat. If your reflexes are not as good as your opponent's, he may be able to grab your foot and throw you off balance. For this reason, a kick should only be utilised in close quarters when your opponent has little to no time to counter. Use your legs as a force to push away more than a force to attack, since real damage to your legs would make escape far more difficult.

Attacking with joints:

Know that your elbows and knees are powerful and focused areas to attack. Utilising your knees and elbows effectively can turn a fight in your favour almost instantly. Aim for nerve centres, such as just below the rib cage, since it can cause a brief spasm which will leave your opponent open to attack.

Vulnerable points: The most venerable points on an opponent are as follows:

Eyes: attack with the fist or fingers to disorientate the opponent.

Ears: Hit with the flat of your hand, and the consequential ringing they hear with disorient them.

Bridge of nose: easy to break, very painful and very distracting.

Chin: kick or elbow this: the chin is tough and will break bones if hit wrong.

Windpipe: An area which can debilitate the opponent easily, but requires great care to avoid severe damage.

Solar plexus: A strong hit here will cause the opponent to be temporarily debilitated.

Groin: I doubt this needs explanation.

Knee: Hitting the back of the knee will cause it to bend, bringing the opponent to their knees.

Instep: Stopping hard on the instep of an opponent prevents them from escaping.

Instruments/Music

Music is a vice not lost on myself; the comforting embrace of the violin guiding me through many any icy London night. The use of an instrument itself does not serve as any great indicator of character; it does not hold inherent strength or intellect. It does, however, connote a skill which begs to be have an audience, and serves as an entrance to any conversation.

SH

139. Long or fake nails on both hands can indicate that the person is not a musician of any nature, as nails can encumber playing most instruments.

140. If a person has deep callouses on the fingers of only one hand, this normally signifies that he plays a stringed instrument.

141. If a person is wearing fairly new looking Converse (you usually tell this by how white the top and sides are) that have the rubber border around the ball of the foot separated from the canvas he is probably in

a marching band, from the bending of back marching and the toe curl of forward marching.

142. A person who usually listens to louder music (like rock) can have more difficulty hearing quieter sounds or music.

143. An avid violinist will usually have a bruise on the left side of the neck.

144. String players have longer fingers on their left hand, and their left fingertips are usually calloused and/or harder than their right.

145. Cellists may have a callous on the outside of their left thumb due to playing thumb position.

146. People who were in marching bands for a long time usually start walking with their left foot. (More noticeably when music they have marched to is playing.)

147. A pianist's hands have well developed muscles and the middle finger tends to curve towards the ring finger.

148. A pianists fingertips will be slightly worn from the constant swiping of keys.

149. If a person's right thumb is crooked or has a callous on the inside, he is likely to play a woodwind instrument like clarinet or saxophone.

150. Note from the above: a callous on the thumb shows experience and dedication to a level where they do not mind long practices without a pad on the thumb rest.

151. A guitarist that has longer nails typically plucks the instrument in favour of using a pick: this is most easily identified on women who are not stereotypically feminine or "masculine" men.

152. Guitarists with roughly cut or damaged nails are likely to be forgetful or to have come to a sudden revelation of the relative ease of playing with short nails. This can make the fingers quite sensitive or even cause them to bleed at times.

153. Musicians who play guitar (bass guitar especially) will not wear rings as they catch on strings and make them buzz.

154. If a person spreads his fingers and the left pinkie is at a greater angle than the other fingers, especially the right pinkie, he is a string player: this is due to the stretch required to reach the 4th fingered note.

155. You can tell how long someone has been playing a reed instrument by how he acts with his reed. If he

soaks it in his mouth just long enough, he us
unused to the taste. If he rolls it around his mouth to
evenly soak both sides, he likely has been playing
for years.

156. If a person has developed the ability to speak
clearly around the reed of an instrument in his
mouth, he has been playing for a long time.

157. Someone who rhythmically moves their fingers
while talking may suggest that he plays an
instrument often.

158. A person who is or has played a wind instrument in
band will often sit at the edge of his or her seat with
impeccable posture, out of habit.

159. When looking at a passage that someone has
written, if his lowercase b's look like musical flats,
it's a good indication that he is a trained musician.

160. Someone whose left shoulder is held higher than his
right likely played the violin or viola through their
developmental years.

161. If a person has been in a marching band for a long
period of time he tends to get in step with whoever
he is walking with without necessarily noticing.

162. People who have been trained to play wind
instruments (such as the flute or clarinet) will

naturally inhale with their stomach or use "diaphragm breathing" keeping their shoulders still.

163. People who play accordion often wear their watch of the right wrist, because the left hand has to go under a strap when playing.

164. Sometimes people may wear a belt buckle to the side if they play an instrument such as a guitar, in order to prevent the buckle from scratching it.

165. Callouses on both hands could indicate guitar playing and/or drum playing.

166. Swollen lips can have a correlation with playing the trumpet/tuba.

167. Of people who have just recently been playing a string instrument, heavy creases will cross the pads of the fingers on the left hand

168. Diagonally going down from the top left to the bottom right of the pad for cello or upright players.

169. Diagonally going from the bottom left to the top left for violin and viola players. (Due to difference in orientation towards the fingerboard.)

170. If a person sits far forward on his chair out of habit but has a noticeable hunch that seems out of place

for their posture, he is likely a musician. (More noticeable for cello players.)

171. A pianist will try to have short nails, as it helps maintain good hand position.

172. Violinists will have a callous on their non-dominant hand, on the last digit of each finger at the 10/11 o'clock position.

173. Musicians are more inclined to misspell the word "triplet" as "tripolet", since this is phonetically how triple notes are counted.

174. A female with a grey/black mark on her upper lip likely plays a brass instrument. This most often appears during menses, but can occur at other times as well.

175. A cellist who has been playing recently may have white marks on his left knee or on the back of his left hand from rosin.

176. A cellist may also have red marks on the inside of the knees as the sides of his instrument may have made an indentation.

Productive Practice

The mind is a muscle. Like any other muscle, it requires regular exercise for it to become stronger. Leave it too long, and it becomes lazy and weak. For a detective, it is often insufficient simply to test memory and observation. This chapter discusses good practices for better thinking.

SH

Activity: Spot the difference.

Description: Admittedly a primitive form of exercise, usually aimed at children. However, the focus this puzzle requires exercises your mind's ability to discern inconsistencies from visual data.

Recommended For: It is an activity which is quick, and easy to do on a regular basis, so it is recommended for those with busy timetables.

Activity: People Watching.

Description: This activity, when done well, should improve observation and subtlety. This entails what you would expect from its title. When in a scenario where you are around people you do not know for an extended period time (trains, buses and cafes are good) spend time observing them. Even if you do not discern any probable deductions, see what you can notice about them. Write a list of what you notice, with things such as what clothes they're wearing, what they have with them, what they want to do. Be aware of people's boundaries and comfort: be clear with them if they notice what you are doing.

Recommended For: People who are stuck in public places for extended periods of time.

Activity: Meditation.

Description: Meditation involves the improvement of concentration and focus. Although it often attributed to religious experiences, it is often used as a way of improving mental abilities. By knowing your own abilities and spending a small period of time every day without distraction, it can help your mental capacities exponentially.

Recommended For: People who have a few minutes to spare in a quiet environment on a fairly regular basis.

Activity: Critical Thinking.

Description: Critical thinking is an essential skill in detective work, particularly when analysing witness' statements. Thinking about credibility and the motive behind written work is an excellent practice of this: the use of any non-fiction for this analysis is adequate, though newspapers are the easiest source of practice.

Recommended For: Advanced readers in need of challenge. Good logic and reasoning are necessary for this activity to be worthwhile.

Activity: Logic based games.

Description: Games are often depicted as a waste of time and of resources, unless they are the likes of chess, draughts, sudoku, crosswords and anagrams. However, work should not become a chore to the worker, the video games of Phoenix Wright, Professor Layton and LA Noire are often cited as "fun" ways to improve logic skills.

Recommended For: Anyone of any age.

Travel

Travel is the greatest technique to expand the mind. It is also necessary for an average lifestyle. The inconsistency in celebration of travel is a bizarre one, drowned in romanticism and logic. Ultimately, everyone travels. The real interest lies in where.

SH

177. If there is a large amount of foreign money in their wallet, they recently been to its country of origin and haven't had time to change it back yet.

178. If a tan line continues under the shirt, they have been in a hotter climate: no one wears a shirt on a sun bed.

179. If a person has an umbrella but hasn't used it in the rain, it is likely the wind is too strong for them to use it.

180. People who take long vacations frequently don't tend to keep house plants.

181. A wallet with slits along the sides of the most easily accessible card slot often belongs to a regular commuter. Thin train tickets do not bulge slots, but can cause frequent small damage.

182. Depending on the country, a tan of the arm which does not match the side that cars drive on (For example, the right in America would mean a tan on the left arm) is an indicator that an individual has done a great deal of driving recently in a sunny area.

183. If it's been snowing for the day and a car is covered in snow it hasn't be used that day. If the windshield has a thinner or non-existing layer of snow, it has been used in the last few hours.

184. A person who is accustomed to carrying a heavy bag will naturally walk tilted towards the opposite side than where he usually carries the bag on his shoulder.

185. A warm car hood on a parked car indicates the car has been in that spot for half an hour or less. (It may be a longer time if the car has a large or inefficient engine.) This is not reliable if the car is left in direct sunlight.

186. With an American, certain words will contain a "z" in the place of an "s" (-ise suffix becomes –ize, for example, realise become realize) -others will contain an "s" in the place of a "c" (-ce suffix becomes -se)

187.-more likely to use "gotten" as opposed to "got".

188.-A British person will spell words with an additional "u" (colour, flavour)

189.-British people may "leave out" the occasional proposition, as well as use single quotation marks in dialogue.

190.-A person from Australia or New Zealand is more likely to use British rules of spelling but may dip into American customs.

191.-European and Asian cultures are more likely to use "British" spellings.

192. Canadian speech and vocabulary choices can be quite similar to American English, but they retain some British spellings, such as colour, favourite and centre.

193. Canadian speech is more likely to use French pronunciations of French derived words such as motif and saboteur.

194. If a person's shoe is more worn on the outer part of the heel, he walks with his toes pointed slightly outwards.

195. If a person instinctively turns the handlebar of a bike to the left after getting off it and locking it he usually drives a moped or a motorcycle.

196. Tourists will walk at a slower pace and tend to be more aware of their surroundings.

197. Someone local to area will be less aware of his surroundings as they know their location well.

198. Tourists pack for perceived weather, often dressed for extremes. They often carry inappropriate clothing with them (such as coats on warm days).

199. If someone has horizontal lines of mud on the back of his knees, it is possible that he traveled by car on a muddy road, and accidentally rubbed the side of the car when getting out.

200. Deviation from the recommended "10 and 2" hand placement during driving can indicate familiarity.

201. A) A local or relaxed driver's hands will be near the bottom of the steering wheel.

202. B) A driver who is anxious, inexperienced or new to the area will have their hands much higher.

203. If someone tends to readjust their car position several times while attempting to park, this might suggest he is a new driver.

204. European men tend to cross their legs when sitting.

205. American men often keep both feet on the ground and apart when sitting.

206. If someone is wearing lighter clothing (t-shirts etc.) during the winter, he may be from a colder climate.

207. Second-generation immigrants may pronounce common word consistently incorrectly, because they were raised by non-native English speakers.

Interrogation

Interrogation, or interview depending on the scenario, can be the element that makes or breaks a case. No matter what series of evidence or theories you have, a poor witness' statement or well-placed lie can make a conviction impossible. Aside from the chapter on lying, there are many elements that should be taken into consideration when interviewing.

SH

<u>Age:</u>
If someone is at the extreme end of the spectrum when it comes to age, it is easy to assume they are not useful to you. This is not the case. Regardless of how young or old, the subject is being interviewed because they have some relevance. Even if you are just corroborating the facts, their input is of some value to you. Like anyone else, they can be unreliable, or secretive for their own means, though in these cases these means are often easy to surpass. For children, they often require comfort or reassurance, though they are by no means new to the concept of bribery. For the elderly, they often know what is expected of them from a situation. Treat them how they want to be treated: approaching them with unnecessary harshness or comfort may be patronising.

Plausibility:
How likely is the given chain of events? My motto
may be "once you have eliminated the impossible,
whatever remains, however improbable, must be the
truth," but it is rare that you have eliminated every
possibility. Know that in many cases, the most
probable answer is also the most likely. (These are,
for the most part, not chronicled simply because the
most probable answer is typically the least
interesting.)

Corroboration:
Do different accounts of the situation match?
Whether it is between different accounts or
evidence, all versions of what happened should
match. Small differences are normal, but the overall
image should be the same. It is very important to
discern how noticeable some details are: memory
retention is never entirely perfect, but should be
accurate to some degree.

Consistency:
Holding many similarities to the above point,
consistency is important between different pieces of
evidence and in a single statement. Lies made
without forethought may lead to inconsistencies in
testimony. If there are inconsistencies in a single
statement, it is not entirely reliable, and needs

further scrutiny. There is a chance that it was a genuine mistake, so tact is necessary to expose whether the blemish is the result of a mistake or memory.

Expertise:
How knowledgeable is the person in question about the subject? If you are interviewing someone about a crime that takes place in a factory, a factory worker is liable to make clearer and more informed statements about it. This can also lead to over-embellishments and assumptions: knowing a large amount about a subject can leave the speaker tempted to speak about the irrelevant.

Vested Interest:
Does the speaker have anything to gain or lose from his testimony? Even if the person in question is innocent of the crime in question, he may have reason to change or withhold information. Does the truth show themself or someone they care about in a bad light? Does it reveal that were lying about something seemingly unrelated? Would they lose money? Would they gain respect? This is similar, but not entirely identical to motive: do they have a reason to present something other than the truth?

Ability to Perceive:

The reliability of a statement can be based entirely upon an individual's ability to perceive the incident in question. The five senses must be called into question: sight, smell, hearing, touch and taste. A majority of cases will disregard smell and taste, but in cases concerning things such as chemicals these things should not be overlooked. Ultimately if the sight or ability to hear is obscured significantly, the information given may not be entirely accurate.

Reputation:
Reputation is the least reliable of influences to judge a statement by. Reputation can, and often is, manipulated to create assumption. Everyone is innocent until proven guilty: regardless of any prior evidence. Reputation is good for finding suspects, but never as evidence of guilt.

Home/Family

There is a reason home is where the heart is.
Nothing bleeds out personality quite like the home.
To inspect the home is to inspect the mind and more
prominently, the habits, of an individual. My own
home is guilty of such a revealing glimpse; through
bullet holes and chemical burns are a less frequent
indication of personality.

SH

208. When at a shared meal, a person who comes from a
large family will look at the quantity he is allowed
compared to the number present instead of
immediately diving in. (Which may happen at big
families with less strict house rules.)

209. If a home's rooms seem crowded with furniture,
then the occupants have moved there from a larger
house.

210. A house has been occupied in the last 24 hours if
brown soil is still in plant pots and/or toothbrushes
are still damp.

211. Recent or current presence of dogs/cats in a home
can be indicated by bite/scratch marks on furniture
and hair clinging to exposed fibrous materials.

212. Dust becomes visible on the surface of liquids left standing for a day or so.

213. Scratches on a lock may mean that the person was shaking when using the key: fear/cold would cause lots of small knicks, while drunkenness would give deep long scratches.

214. Light fixtures are almost always centred to a room or to a piece of furniture. If the lighting is not centred to either, the room was recently redone.

215. You can tell if someone has been using an electrical appliance recently by its temperature. A recently used appliance will be warm, losing heat as time passes.

216. If a young child has turn ups on their trousers and/or wears a belt, the trousers are likely to be second hand; not fitted.

217. American accents differ depending on their specific area of origin. Someone from the North will typically pronounce the "ar" sound as "ah". Their "r's" will be more emphasised. Someone from the more Southern states typically draws out their vowels and is "lazy" on letters like "r".

218. Educated Americans generally pride themselves on not having regional accents, meaning that regional accents can be a class indicator but not always.

219. A person who habitually leaves items out of the fridge has a high probability of having recently departed from a communal living situation where meals are served in a cafeteria or hall.

220. Many uncommon physical traits- red hair, curved thumbs etc. - are inherited through a recessive gene. People of different generations which share a rare gene are more likely to be related.

221. You can tell something about a person's native language by telling them to write something in gibberish: the consistency of long and short words tells what their native language consists of.

222. A clear area on an otherwise messy desk can indicate a space where something was taken hurriedly: most often a laptop.

223. If someone frequently speaks louder than is appropriate, it is possible they spend a lot of time in a loud environment.

224. (Supposedly) The youngest child is more likely to have a personality that will attract a lot of attention, possibly due to trying to compete against siblings for attention.

225. If you find a large number of mugs around the house of a person, they are likely to drink mostly hot drinks such as tea, coffee and hot chocolate.

226. If someone's house has dirt collected under surfaces, it is likely they care more for appearances than health.

227. Someone who has been deprived of food in the past will make sure that food is always in their immediate environment.

228. People from small towns are more likely to interact with people they pass, while people from large cities tend to maintain a lesser level of interaction.

229. If someone has basic childcare skills without having any children, it is likely he is an older sibling. The larger the age gap the more skills they tend to have.

230. Frantic attempts to take fur off othes suggests the person does not own a pet, but has recently been in contact with an animal.

231. If a bathtub or sink has discolouring in it, it indicates it has not been cleaned/used in a long time.

232. If you make a quick movement towards any animal and it shows submissive behaviour, it is possible they were formerly abused.

233. When looking to deduce from objects in their space, there are three basic steps you should take:

234. A) First, determine what the object is and what its purpose it. (Such as a desk calendar showing that he cares about being organised to some extent.)

235. B) Second, examine the state of the object. (Continuing with the desk calendar, how full is it? Is it maintained?)

236. C) Lastly, look at the position of the object, or its place in context of the person in question. (For example, photographs facing in suggest sentimentality, photographs facing out suggest a display.)

237. If a person is very untidy it may be difficult to determine what in his work space is more or less relevant to your observations: focus on ease of access to items in these situations.

238. A person who is trying to hide a physical object in a room will often try to "block" it with his body or lead you as far away as possible from it.

239. In an emergency, such as a fire, people will naturally gravitate towards that which holds most value to them in an instinct to protect it. (This may not be as severe as actually trying to recover it, it can be limited to just looking in the object's direction.)

240. A way to tell if someone has recently been in a darkened house is by touching the light bulbs. Many light bulbs emit excessive heat when turned on, leaving them warm to the touch for 5 or more minutes after they have been switched off. This is dependent upon the efficiency of the lights and how long they were turned on.

241. You can tell how recently a piano has been used by the dust on the keys. The most commonly used keys are typically the ones in the middle, so check those first.

242. You can also tell how recently used a piano is by playing the same note in different octaves to test whether it is in tune or not.

243. The contents of someone's fridge can indicate a great deal about them. Some indicative aspects are: the tidiness of shelves, the nutritional value of the items, the presence/lack of alcohol, takeout boxes etc.

244. A well-used video game controller is likely to have faded colours on the buttons and where held due to friction and sweat.

245. Someone who owns pets will typically extend his hand and allow an animal to sniff it before petting

them, allowing the animal to get to know them and reduce the risk of the animal lashing out.

246. Dishes and glasses that have been rinsed but not washed (shown through "cloudy" glass) and put back on the shelf suggest the person is tidy and doesn't have guests over often.

247. People tend to revert to their native language when yelling in anger.

248. Note from above, that people even revert to native accent when yelling in anger.

249. Uneven skincare on the face suggests the person may have a mirror which is fixed to the wall, giving him a limited view.

250. Note that this could also be an indicator of poor vision in one eye and being in a rush to get ready.

251. Hanging clothes outside and using "low temperature" laundry detergent indicates environmental awareness.

252. However, hanging clothes outside and using low value laundry detergent merely also indicates frugality.

Crime Scene Investigation

Crime Scene Investigation is often the very first impression given of a crime. Proper knowledge of suitable behaviour and checks at a crime scene are vital, regardless of one's role in investigation. The following advice is far from comprehensive: consider it merely as a starting point for better investigation.

SH

Time sensitive data:
Time is of the essence with any and all crime scenes. Other than the obvious need to catch the culprit as soon as possible, many pieces of evidence can be rendered almost useless due to the passage of time. Organic matter (not limited to the human body) can decay and decompose with alarming speed, regardless of the condition in which it is kept. (Unless it is free of oxygen, where decomposition cannot take place.) Other elements, such as temperature, weather and exposure, can threaten all evidence: efficiency is necessary. Such time pressure can lead to poor assumptions and missed clues, so do not bow to it. A balance between pace and thorough searching must be established.

Establishing information:

For consultants or investigators who are of a higher of specialised level, information may be given beforehand. A copy of key facts which have been ascertained prior to arrival is quite common: the victim and any professional opinions being a top priority. However, there are those who have not yet ascended to such a level of being handed information. They have the requirement of finding it for themselves: ensuring no-one interferes with the scene and speaking to any witnesses. Establishing a sense of calm or control will make investigation much easier.

Crowd control:

As detrimental as the police can be to the maintenance of a crime scene, civilians are even worse. Beyond the destruction of evidence, people have a terrible tendency toward misinterpretation of facts. The presence of police creates an atmosphere of paranoia and panic. A simple police tape represents a line from the comfortable to a place of danger. But this danger is nonspecific: anything ranging from a robbery to a homicide is the concern of police. Utilise the police for this: keep onlookers away. Anyone who is unrelated to the crime in question can only be a nuisance who must be kept away.

Trauma:
There is one important factor to consider, regardless
of experience and ability: you are human. The
witnesses, victims, even other detectives: they are
all human. Crime scenes can be horrific places,
filled with the full extent of human cruelty. Take
note of tolerance of these things, and the appropriate
levels of exposure to individuals. Victims should be
exposed to traumatic elements as little as possible:
the fastest way to isolate them from you is to make
them uncomfortable. Detectives should have some
stomach for it, but even they have limits. Know
them, and you will get the best quality work from
them.

Post mortem:
Quite obviously only relevant to murder cases, post
mortem is the process of examining the body to
determine the cause of death. A majority of murders
have clear causes which can be determined at the
scene: blunt force trauma creates bruises and the use
of a piercing weapon will cause extensive bleeding
in a focused point. Blood itself is also a major
indicator of the situation in which the murder took
place. For example, if there is an absence of blood
at the scene while there is blood on the body, the
body may have moved from where the act took
place. Alternatively, if there is blood at the scene

and none on the body, it is likely the blood belongs to someone else. The amount of time that has passed can be hazarded from this information too: such as blood on material turning brown after 30 minutes. Overall, post mortem is the most reliable and detailed source of information on the body. It will take time, but the post mortem report must be consulted through the course of investigation.

Miscellaneous

A detective must be prepared for all possible demands from the crime scene. What do you expect me to write for this? You've literally given me an adjective to work from. The others were a stretch but now you have exceeded my limit. And safely in the knowledge that you have left it so late to contact me that you will not read this except for the first and last sentences, I am content in rambling nonsense of a similar calibre to your research. Therefore, the miscellaneous cannot be miscounted.

SH

253. Look where the bank card is in the wallet: as the most used, it will be with any other contents of the wallet which are used often.

254. A pink or red palm indicates that a person has been carrying something heavy by a handle or handhold within the past 15-20 minutes.

255. If a person has jeans that are the right length and yet ragged around the bottom, it suggests that they haven't had a significant growth spurt within the past year.

256. Someone who holds his or her wallet/purse in the front pocket is most likely overly protective or paranoid due to the fact the money is where they

feel most able to protect it. If this is the case, other items of value may be kept in the front pockets.

257. If a person has fake nails, she may have a phone with a keyboard (For example, A Blackberry). She probably won't use a touch screen since the nails make it difficult to operate efficiently.

258. A person who spends a lot of time on the computer, or a less social person will blink considerably less than a social individual.

259. Grass seeds and/or dirt on the interior of a shoe indicates that the owner removed them for a period while still outside and then put them back on again.

260. A person who has recently dyed his hair will often have trace amounts of the dye on the skin, mostly at the hairline. Typically more so if he dyed it himself instead of having a professional dye it.

261. One can tell whether a sock was worn on the right foot or the left door by the indentation left by the big toe. Also, the curved indentation of the foot's front pad will peak closer to the big toe's side.

262. People generally write slightly higher than their eye level when writing on a wall or chalkboard.

263. People who type on phone or computer keyboards and touch screens regularly will have a flatter thumb than those who don't.

264. Narcissists often word sentences with the subject as themselves. (For example, "I like ice cream" rather than "ice cream is good".)

265. A) Narcissists often assume all people they like or respect share their opinions and those they don't like do not. (For example, an intelligent fan of Sherlock Holmes books might assume all intelligent people like Sherlock Holmes books.)

266. B) Even narcissists who do not consider themselves attractive will watch their reflections.

267. Handwriting style can change relative to mood: less focus due to strong emotions like anger can make writing sloppier.

268. People may not wear dark clothing to avoid showing the shedding of pale hair or signs of dry skin.

269. Dark clothing may be avoided if a person easily overheats, possibly from being used to a colder climate.

270. Those who read frequently at a high level are more likely to use advanced language in the correct context, but mispronounce it.

271. A person who is casually reading through a book usually turns one page using a forefinger or middle finger first, carefully turning one page at a time. You can tell if a person is hastily reading through a book if he flips through the page with pressure on their middle finger.

272. When using a higher quality digital camera in low light, it can be assumed that, if the photographer uses the built in flash, they have little or no formal training in the use of said camera and are probably shooting on automatic.

273. If the toes on a person's shoes are particularly worn, it suggests that the wearer drags his feet when he walks.

274. You can tell a person sits below the appropriate height of his computer (due to inappropriate seating) if his dominant hand has a softened point of skin on the underside of it.

275. People who openly criticise themselves out loud fall into two categories. Commonly, a person criticizing his appearance is usually searching for compliments. Otherwise he has low self-esteem: but

this is much rarer since this is not something that's not generally accepted.

276. One can tell the reason behind tattoos by looking at their purpose: particularly with text. If the reader can read it by looking down, it was done for personal enjoyment. If it is upside down for the wearer but readable for the observer, it is meant to give the wearer their desired image.

277. Males tend to use fewer emoticons/text faces in comparison to females.

278. When a person sleeps with blankets over his head at night, it can often mean that he is self-conscious or easily frightened.

279. Older men tend to wear tie clips lower on their shirts than younger men: those who care about their age may wear their tie clip higher.

280. You can tell how much time a person spends at his computer by the amount of clutter that accumulates near it. Used dishes especially suggest that the owner rarely leaves the keyboard.

281. Someone who has short hair but carries hairbands around with him likely had long hair until recently, not yet bothering to remove the hair bands from his person.

282. If someone has long hair and carries hairbands it is possible they do activities that involved a lot movement so they want their hair out of the way.

283. Discoloured nails can be due to hair dye, for example, nails can be stained yellow/orange if using henna to dye one's own or helping dye another's hair.

284. Someone who has worn toes on their shoes might be quite clumsy and bump their toes against things a lot (possibly due to poor hand-eye coordination or a growth spurt.)

285. A black ring (or sometimes a ring with a black stone) worn on the middle finger of the right hand is often used as a symbol for asexuality.

286. You can see if a watch is a gift by the shoes worn at the same time: if the watch is expensive and the shoes are cheap the watch is likely a gift.

287. If the watch is cheap and the clothes are expensive the watch most likely holds sentimental value.

288. If someone wears a watch but asks for the time rather than looking at it, they may have only acquired the watch recently.

289. If the skin at the corners of a person's fingernails are a strange colour, then it is possible that person has been finger painting.

290. Fake blood on material will remain red after 30 minutes.

291. Real blood on material will turn brown after 30 minutes.

292. If a person has round scabs or blisters on the back of each heel it means that he has new boots which don't quite fit.

293. Even if someone's shoes fit well, a large amount of walking can cause blisters due to excessive sweating.

294. If someone has on a class ring and he is in his thirties or older, they probably reminisce about their college days: possibly a reminder of a better time for them.

295. A woman with short and usually straight hair will not carry a brush: it is unlikely that she needs to brush her hair regularly since it is low maintenance.

296. A person with a tan that reaches to or past their knee but not into the crease behind their knee has spent most of his time outside sitting.

297. You can tell how clumsy someone may be by their mobile phone.

298. If there are cracks in the screen and dents on the plastic they can be used to track the point of impact when dropped.

299. Discolouration on a screen shows damaged pixels.

300. A Claddagh ring is not always an accurate sign of someone's relationship: they are often worn more for fashion than tradition.

301. Due to their training, Scouts often shake with their left hand.

302. It is quite common for people who use sign language regularly to wear their watches on the non-dominant hand facing inwards, allowing them to check the time easily while talking.

303. Note this is also true of guitarists.

304. A body is never beyond recognition. Each person's ear is unique and can be used to identify the victim.

305. Often you can tell if a person is male or female by their elbows: a man's typically point more backwards whereas a woman's elbows point more to the sides

306. Callouses on the fingers, especially at the base of the pinkie and on the side of the index finger near the top knuckle, could be the result of frequently winding and unwinding a heavy power or extension cord.

307. If a belt is slightly on the side it might mean that it is the wrong size. If it's too long, by shifting the buckle on the side, the belt it reaches the loops in the back, otherwise the part in excess hangs loose. It's possible the person lost weight recently.

308. A listener who is merely touching his face (for example, index finger to his forehead or lips) is listening attentively and thinking.

309. A listener who is touching his face *and* resting his head (for example thumb under chin, index finger pointed up) is less likely to be paying attention.

310. If a person has a single yellow/orange stained fingernail, he has most likely been peeling an orange or Satsuma with his bare hands.

311. Depending on how organised someone's school book/binder is, you can tell the extent to which they care about the class.

312. When walking women have their steps centred at their hips with minimal movement from their upper bodies.

313. When walking, men tend to move more in their torso and shoulders.

314. People typically are aware of what their upper body is conveying in terms of body language, defensive behaviour can be seen in the position of their legs despite this. (Such as crossed legs.)

315. Someone who constantly puts his hands on his chest right below his collarbone is using a feminine act that shows a sense of self-protection in moments of uneasiness like shielding oneself.

316. If an American high school student has a schedule which becomes incredibly busy during the months of January and February, and he is often absent or late in the week during spring, he is are likely part of a robotics team.

317. When examining something handwritten, if the words are squashed together at the end of the page it has been rushed.

318. If something handwritten has consistent spacing and sized letters, it is clear the writer was thinking ahead about what he was writing and that his words were likely prepared.

319. The environment in which a laptop has been used can be indicated by stains/materials (paint, sawdust, dirt, food etc.) found on the charger cable or bottom

of the laptop, which is often encouraged due to the fact they overheat.

320. If someone leans on his elbows often and for extended periods of time the skin on them will often be slightly rough (and red if recent).

321. A) If this mark is only on one elbow it is likely his non-dominant hand if he was working while leaning on his elbow.

Disguise

Watson has frequently commented on my abilities
in disguise, often claiming he was utterly unable to
detect my true identity on multiple occasions. This
suggests two things, the first being that Watson is
criminally inattentive or prone to hyperbole.
(Something that is not entirely surprising...) The
second observation is that disguise is more than just
a passing interest in my line of work. It is often
essential in obtaining information or avoiding
detection, and thus must be treated seriously.

                                                      SH

The key elements of disguise are as follows:

Facial Features:
This is typically considered the most recognisable
aspect of the body, though this is merely because it
is the first feature noticed in regular conversation.
The face is unlike a finger print: aspects blend and
become indistinguishable. A nose is the same for all
people unless special measures are taken to notice
minute differences. This is necessary when

imitating another person, but otherwise not needed. Changing just one feature such as eye colour or severity of cheekbones will likely throw suspicion off for a majority of people. Conceal distinguishing features, such as freckles and scars: the most basic arsenal of makeup will suffice for this.

Clothing:
Even for those untrained in deduction, clothing presents certain assumptions. It composes the majority of your appearance, likely the only part a person will able to recall. Here is the best place to consider the term of "hiding in plain sight": uniforms, high visibility jackets and lanyards indicate some kind of authority that most will not question. Keep note of smaller details: follow the crowd of any job, take note of any rules they must obey. Make sure your cleanliness correlates to what you wish be: for example, someone who wears tattered clothes is associated with hard labour or homelessness and is unlikely to have clean hands.

Body Language:
This is arguably the most important factor in any disguise. In many scenarios, mere confidence is enough to bypass security without the need for costume. As said previously, people will rarely challenge a source of clear authority. Someone with extensive knowledge of the situation is not always a

source of authority: a few small truths (name dropping, layout, equipment etc.) can hide any bluffing from scrutiny. Confidence is all that is truly required: eye contact, wide stance and clear voice. Frequently, it is seen as more than someone's job is worth to conflict with the interests of a loud and certain guest, regardless of whether he is expected. Equally, attempting to garner sympathy requires the opposite: unfocused, taking up as little space as possible, stumbling and hesitant speech.

Context:
Preparation is vital when planning on disguising yourself. No matter how skilled you become in the art of disguise, there is always a chance of encountering questions and this where context is needed. Waiting until questioned to establish a context is a guarantee for disaster: always plan ahead. A full context doesn't need too much information, only enough that feels natural. Trying to remember an overly complicated context is a waste of time and effort. Typically, a context will only require a name and a reason for being where you are. Any additional detail should be divined only from the most likely questions you would be asked if discovered.

Health

Admittedly, the true expert in this field is my companion, Dr Watson. He is fortunate enough to not be worth waving leverage over, so the author of this particular book did not invite him to divulge his expertise. In light of this, it should be noted that the job of the detective is not to diagnose: more often than not health is used as an alibi rather than anything else. Observation alone is not enough to diagnose, nor enough to establish certainty. This is a minefield of such things.

SH

322. When somebody's eyes show many blood vessels or seem to be irritated, it may not be due to crying: it can be a product of dry eyes. This can be caused by extended use of screens, contact with smoke or frequent use of an air conditioner.

323. Piercings always leave marks or scars; the more recently the piercing was removed, the more prominent the mark.

324. A person who has used a cane for a long time will sustain an uneven stance for several months later.

325. Dark rings under the eyes and no other signs of lack of sleep may indicate the person has allergies which have been troubling him lately.

326. If someone wears long sleeved shirts in the summer he is likely trying to hide his arms from being seen. This is often to hide things such as tattoos or scars.

327. A smallpox vaccination is usually given in the shoulder, and is common in anyone born before 1977.

328. If someone has a smallpox vaccine scar but was born after 1977, he probably spent time abroad in the military or in countries where the disease has not been eradicated.

329. Some people may be tired although they do not bear obvious physical signs of it. Losing their train of thought, being unable to articulate what they mean to say, staring off into space, or a general lack of interest can be indicative of a lack of sleep.

330. If a person has had an injury that caused any amount of trauma, he may subconsciously touch the part of the body that was injured, even if it has long healed.

331. If someone needs glasses to focus on a distant objects, he is near sighted; if he needs them to see close objects, he is farsighted.

332. If a person uses a cane and pushes off it slightly when he walks, he most likely has a joint injury where putting weight on the joint is painful. If he doesn't push off it with each step, he most likely uses it to aid balance, due to a problem that is more likely muscular or nervous based.

333. If a person uses a cane and the cane is wooden/coloured/of fixed length, the injury/disability is likely long term.

334. If a person uses a cane and the cane is made of metal and of adjustable height and has a generic "candy cane" grip, it's probably a short-term one issued by a hospital.

335. People suffering from the mental disorder OCD become anxious or agitated when someone is doing something they would like to fix, but can't.

336. You can tell if someone has hearing problems in one ear if his head is more inclined to a certain angle, to compensate for lack of hearing.

337. It is possible to tell if someone is far sighted if he is looking at the text with his head tilted upwards

because he is used to using the most magnifying part of the glasses, the bottom.

338. A person with scoliosis (curvature of the spine) will often have more pronounced muscles on one side of the spine, and may have uneven hips, shoulders and leg length.

339. People with scoliosis often have a "rolling" gait.

340. People with scoliosis near their nick will often hold their head tilted to the side opposite to the curve in their back.

341. Small, round scars are usually not from accidental injuries- they indicate small, intentional burns or picking of skin.

342. A person who habitually breathes through his mouth may suggest he is prone to sinus infections/nasal issues.

343. If one shoe is significantly more worn than the other, the person may have been wearing a cast/brace for an extended period of time.

344. People who have a hearing problem tend to stand nearer to the person talking and they also concentrate more on the hearing.

345. People who have bad hearing talk louder than necessary and look at people's lips when talking.

346. Discoloured nails may be a sign of fungal infection.

347. Some people suffering from continual anxiety begin to pick at their skin when feeling anxious, often locating it to one area, such as their arms or head.

348. Someone over the age of 50 with a heavy limp on one side but no recent injuries may have suffered from polio as a child.

349. Pulling at eyebrow hair, eyelashes and even head hair can be a sign of trichotillomania, a compulsion to pull out one's own hair, however this is relatively unlikely.

350. Russell's sign is when cuts, bruises or callouses appear on a person's knuckles: this can be an indicator of stimulating the throat to encourage vomiting.

351. Woman have different symptoms of heart attack from men, often feeling symptoms similar to indigestion and heartburn.

352. A person who sneezes/sniffles frequently and has a chafed nose is sick.

353. This differs from someone who has an allergy, as he tends to be better prepared to handle his sneezing without chafing.

354. Rigor mortis sets in 3-8 hours after death, and passes after 36-48 hours due to decomposition.

355. A body will become cold after approximately 8-36 hours. Factors that impact this include body size (larger bodies cool slower) and the temperature of surroundings (a warmer environment results in slower cooler.)

356. Coffee and cigarettes may be used as a form of appetite suppressant, which is seen mostly among dancers.

357. If someone has had IV in the recent past there is likely to be indicative bruise of scar where it was, most commonly on the back of the hand, the crook of the elbow or the wrist: the location changes depending on where a good vein can be found.

358. Lack of sleep results in wrinkles around the edges and bottoms of the eyes, regardless of age.

359. If someone wears through his shoes under the balls of his feet, they may have a shortened Achilles tendon. When the Achilles tendon is too short, the muscles in the leg force the foot to put on weight on the toes/ball of the foot in order to compensate.

360. Note on the above, other signs are the person's feet may "wobble" outwards when they walk, or collapse inwards.

More Questions for Sherlock

Q: *Did you hate school when you went through it?*
A: Who doesn't?
SH

Q: *What's your opinion on revenge?*
A: Overrated, overused and under developed.
SH

Q: *Do you think you'd be able to commit the perfect murder?*
A: I know I could.
Luckily Moriarty and I fell into different circles.
SH

Q: *We are discovered. Flee immediately.*
A: An excellent attempt, but I am not the one in five.
I have no intention of leaving.
SH

Q: *How do you make the perfect cup of tea?*
A: Step 1: Obtain a landlady or Watson.
Step 2: Demand tea.

Step 3 (if necessary): Escalate scale of experiment to the point endangering self.
Step 4: Be given tea.
Step 5: Repeat.
SH

Q: *Do you have a preference when it comes to forms of government?*
A: So long as they do not interfere with me and keep Mycroft occupied, I do not care.
SH

Q: *Have you ever been in love?*
A: Why would that matter?
SH

Q: *Who started the feud between you and Mycroft?*
A: Mycroft.
SH
(Author's note: When asked, Mycroft insisted it was Sherlock.)

Q: *Would you want to be able to read people's minds?*
A: It is harder to prove to people that I can't.
SH

Q: *What do you do when you're bored?*
A: Shoot, smoke and study.
SH

Q: *Why did you become a detective?*
A: A combination of boredom and frustration.
SH

Q: *What were your parents like?*
A: They were supportive, in their minds.
SH

Q: *Is analysing handwriting worthwhile?*
A: It quite depends on the situation.
Graphology rarely leads to insights into psyche that
people expect.
However, handwriting can be linked back to
individuals in certain scenarios.
SH

Q: *What is your favourite phrase?*
A: Not "Elementary my dear Watson."
I'm not certain how that rumour started.
SH

Q: *What is your favourite piece of clothing?*
A: Not the deerstalker hat.
Again, not certain how that rumour began.
SH

Q: *Who is your favourite criminal?*

A: Having a favourite criminal would be rather like having a favourite toothache.
SH

Handedness

The cornerstone of deduction, often the defining factor in an investigation, is handedness of the person in question. It may seem trivial and bizarre to the novice of deduction, and yet that is the way of humanity. A left-handed man cannot shoot the right side of his own head. A writing hand in plaster may rule out any involvement in activity, criminal or otherwise. Our hands are instruments with which we manipulate the world, and overlooking them is akin to overlooking the world itself.

SH

361. An indent or lump on the middle finger of the hand indicates the person writes a lot with that hand.

362. Greyish or blackish marks on the little finger of the writing hand implies the person has been writing recently: soft marks are pencil, darker inky marks are pen.

363. If a person has a callous on the inside of the middle finger it shows where they tightly grip a pencil or pen when writing.

364. Avid artists usually have trace amount of their materials left on the cuff of their sleeves, more so on the dominant hand.

365. You can tell what hand is dominant if the person is wearing nail polish: the neater quality is on the non-dominant hand.

366. Several lines or streaks of faint reddish skin or discolouration on the outer side of the non-dominant hand shows she may have been testing different cosmetics recently.

367. Take note of how a person's fingers and hands curl as they walk. People that have been carrying things generally continue to "carry" them for hours after due to muscle memory.

368. You can tell if someone is left- or right-handed by looking at the space bar, the side most worn down matches their dominant hand. (For example, if they are right handed, the right side would be worn down.)

369. Slight diagonal creases in the corner of a piece of paper suggest that whoever has been writing on the paper keeps the paper on a slant to write, and the paper has been pressed between the arm and the surface he is writing against. If the creases are on the left side, he is right-handed and vice versa. The more vertical the creases are, it suggests the paper is more tilted.

370. You can tell what hand a person writes with by the pocket they keep their mobile phone/favoured electronic device.

371. A person will usually, but not always, kick with the foot opposite to the hand they write with. (For example, Right handed people typically kick with their left.)

372. In approximately a 75 percent majority, people wear their watch on their non-dominant hand.

373. A person is more likely to wear bulkier jewellery on their non-dominant hand.

374. People who have experience with children will generally carry kids on their non-dominant side so their dominant hand is free.

375. Artists typically have graphite "smudged" on their middle fingertip from blending, or possibly on their forefinger from holding the pencil lead down to sketch.

376. Professional or experienced artists usually blend using equipment rather than their fingers.

377. Left-handed people often have more defined signs of pen or graphite on the side of their hand from writing and dragging their hands across the written page.

378. When falling forward, a person would prevent hitting the floor by stopping himself with his foot. If a person places his right foot forward first (to stop him from falling), it would show he is right handed, and vice-versa.

379. Left-handed people tend to sit on the leftmost seat on a table.

380. Left-handed people may go out of their way to sit to the left of right-handed people to avoid clashing arms when writing or eating.

381. People tend to cross their arms so their dominant hand is tucked into their body.

382. Right-handed people will generally draw things facing left and vice versa.

383. When applying a pin, a right handed person will attach their pin on their left side and vice versa.

384. A) If not, it is very likely someone else put their pin on.

385. When in a clapping audience you can often tell who is left or right handed based on how they clap- a right handed person will clap right hand onto left hand and vice versa.

386. If a person is right-handed, his supplies or pens will be typically kept to his right for ease of access.

387. [Supposedly] you can tell whether someone is left or right handed by looking at their "jaw muscles." If the left side of the jaw is more prominent, it implies he is left handed, due to the way he puts food in his mouth.

Common Codes

Codes have been essential to both detectives and criminals alike for many years. They have meant the difference between life and death on multiple occasions and must be treated with such respect. Some codes have become the backbone of modern communication, such as Morse and binary. Others are less available, and should be investigated with continual dedication to keep all information freely available.

SH

Morse Code:

This is a universal code which conveys information as series of on-off tones, lights or clicks as either dots or dashes. The length of a dot is one unit of time, while a dash is three units, with a space of one unit between the parts of one letter. The space between letters is three units and the space between words is seven units. It was frequently used for sending telegraphs.

A	.-	J	.---	S	...	2	..---
B	-...	K	-.-	T	-	3	...--
C	-.-.	L	.-..	U	..-	4	....-
D	-..	M	--	V	...-	5	.....
E	.	N	-.	W	.--	6	-....
F	..-.	O	---	X	-..-	7	--...
G	--.	P	.--.	Y	-.--	8	---..
H	....	Q	--.-	Z	--..	9	----.
I	..	R	.-.	1	.----	0	-----

Examples:

SOS: ... --- ...
Hurry: .... ..- .-. .-. -.—
Murder: -- ..- .-. -.. . .-.
Stop: ... - --- .--.
Baker Street: -... .- -.- . .-.   ... - .-. . . —

Gate Codes:

Somewhat similar to Morse code, this is a visual replacement of letters with an alternative image: in this case a basic pattern of gates with dots in them.

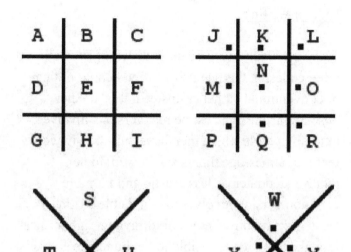

Examples:

SOS: ∨ E ∨

Hurry: ⊓ < ⌐ ⌐ <

Murder: ∃ < ⌐ ⊐ □ ⌐

Stop: ∨ > E ⊓

Baker Street: ⊔ ⌟ ⊔ □ ⌐ ∨ > ⌐ □ □ >

<u>Hidden Writing:</u>

Many consider this to be quite different from all other codes, in that the text is often kept to ordinary or conventional alphabet. Instead, it is merely obscured from sight. Some real versions involve tattooing words which then have hair grown over them, or a message that is swallowed: to be regurgitated later. A less drastic and far more common version involves an "invisible writing." Many inks require the use of ultraviolet light or heat to make them really visible to the human eye: this is true even of common replacements for invisible ink, the most common of which being lemon juice. There are even codes which hide within text, yet to be deciphered from the bulk of content: for example, using the first letter of each line.

Crime/Lying

Honesty may be brutal, yet there is such an insistence on ignoring it, one can only find value in it. Crime may not be my calling and yet an in-depth knowledge of its contrast is essential to prevent it. In some ways I am thankful for that. In others I wish they would be just an iota more intelligent.

SH

388. If a person blinks less than 2 times per minute, it is a sign of nerves, possibly from lying or anti-social habits.

389. A person usually makes a lot of gestures when telling a true story, when telling a lie a person's hands will stay noticeably still.

390. A smashed window will always leave glass on the side opposite to the place of impact.

391. If someone is lying to you, he is more likely to look you directly in the eyes after speaking in an attempt to dissuade you or check to see if you are "buying their story." Experienced liars are better at maintaining this gaze while telling lies.

392. Contradictions are the most common way to expose lies: additional querying to reveal contradictions is

far from impossible. Cover stories are usually quite rigid in the way they are presented: right down to wording in some cases.

393. Liars often respond with longer, more rambling sentences.

394. The word "never" is frequently relied upon in deception, especially when questioning is led with the word "ever". For example, "Ever been to 42nd Street?" "Never even heard of it."

395. Liars tend to divulge unnecessary detail, often small truths, in order to make their story more persuasive.

396. Premeditated lies are those which are long, detailed and insistent: those told without prior planning are often much easier to reveal through questioning.

397. [Supposedly] Liars are more likely to touch their face when lying as part of a consistent sense of morality.

398. Liars are likely to tug at their collars or scratch at their necks because lying increases blood pressure around the neck.

399. Movements will often be restricted and small, as liars try to overcompensate and hide any revealing "tells".

400. Liars will often take up "defensive" body language when telling lies. For example, crossing their arms.

401. The letter "e" is the most used one in the English language. When cracking a secret code, the one symbol that appears the most is likely "e."

402. If you are talking to someone who has hidden something you're looking for, talk to them about the object or create an illusion of immediate danger. People will usually look at the spot where they have hidden it as reflex.

403. When someone is hiding something, move around the room. Even if you are talking about a different topic, they will subconsciously try to get between you and the hiding place, or become uncomfortable when you get close to it.

404. Someone who wears glasses and adjusts them frequently may do so to relieve stress, nerves or hide the fact he is lying.

405. Liars subconsciously raise the pitch of their voice slightly.

406. Statistics show a person is more likely to cry for help when threatened by a gun than when threatened by a knife. This is due to the threat of pain rather than death being more prevalent with knifes.

407. A) If someone is forced somewhere without any clear sign of struggle, it is more likely to be with a knife.

408. Incorporating yourself into another person's lie is the easiest way to confirm if there is one. If someone claims to be somewhere they were not, and you remark you saw them there, they are likely to agree without hesitation. You lie reflects theirs and they cannot protest it without revealing their own. (The best way to reveal deceit is to change small but significant details they attest to and see if they notice.)

409. A person who is lying will become anxious if you continually refute him: an honest person is more likely to become frustrated or angry.

410. In a close-knit community, the theft of an item that is usually displayed (such as a doormat or garden figures) should be considered a statement, since there is little financial gain and no way to display their findings.

411. Liars tend to use "distancing" language or stiff repetition in order to stick to their established story.

412. The inability to make eye contact does not mean that someone is lying in all cases, particularly if it is a difficult or uncomfortable truth.

413. Contact with a person's elbow (even in a friendly
     manner) is a good neutral way to throw a person off,
     preventing him from lying with as much ease, since
     it is an uncommon and unexpected form of
     interaction.

Research

I have said in the past that the mind is like an attic: capable of holding much, but not everything. As such, there will be cases encountered where the detective, no matter how knowledgeable, will be required to conduct research. Research is hardly the most glamourous aspect of the detective and is frequently cited as the most uninteresting activity in which to partake. However, high-quality research is absolutely necessary to create a strong arsenal against crime.

SH

Sourcing:
Any information, regardless of whether it is of academic and social origin, requires sources. You must know where the information comes from for everything you work upon. Police will require the sources in an official legal capacity outside of your own need for context. Other than that, you must consider the reliability of your sources. See the details listed in the interrogation section to see how reliable your source is: does he or she have any reasons to mislead you? Finding multiple sources for information is both necessary and the best way to establish the accuracy of your information. Note that simply being from a newspaper or book is

never a guarantee for reliability: question everything,

Books:
Using books for research is, as mentioned, not always reliable for information. However, learning to use them for efficient research is absolutely necessary. Create your own collection of useful volumes, organised in a way which is natural to your own sense of knowledge seeking. (Unless you naturally follow alphabetical or Dewy Decimal systems, the frequency of use or topic is the best way to organise books.) Mark key points and earmark vital pages: buying books second hand often does much of this for view. Caution is advised with the purchase of second-hand books however: missing pages, obscured text and idiotic annotations can only slow investigation.

Online:
The internet is notorious for being simultaneously the fastest source for information and the most unreliable. The mantra of "don't believe everything you read" is absolutely necessary here, since quite literally anyone with access to the internet can write on it. Finding multiple sources for information is thankfully quite simple due to search engines, but many of the more... unsavoury details will prove almost impossible to find through such conventional

means. Note that some subjects are deemed serious enough to incur surveillance if you were to use the internet to find them, so exercise limits.

Assistance:
The Baker Street Irregulars are my typical resource for more personal investigations. I am fortunate enough to have the resources to pay for the services of a large group of people to follow elements of my investigation. For those who cannot recruit bands of people to do surveillance, there are many ways to gain assistance without those involved being aware of it. Ingratiating yourself into an affected group with appropriate levels of empathy is good way to gain information directly from those involved. While this removes any risk of misreported information from agents of yours, there is still no guarantee that the source itself is reliable. Ultimately, all forms of assistance must be held to the same level of scrutiny as any conventional source of information.

Emotion and Interaction

Contrary to popular opinion, emotion is not the enemy of reason. Often, emotion is the accomplice. It is a crowbar in the window frame of reason, if you will. It offers more truth than many words can, showing betrayal and agony that would never be willingly pried from the mouth. Interaction is what separates us from animals, supposedly. I have yet to pinpoint how our body language truly differs.

SH

414. Dilated eyes can indicate arousal or interest.

415. If a person's jaw locks, it can be a result of subconsciously grinding the teeth, possibly from stress.

416. To find out where someone is keeping something, tell them yours has been stolen. He will automatically check the whereabouts of his.

417. People don't like silence will often rush to fill it; if you're asking someone a question, you can get him to talk more about it by keeping quiet.

418. You can tell if a person if "truly smiling" by the number of muscles moving in his face: his eyes and nose will "crinkle".

419. [Supposedly] You can tell what someone is thinking by where his eyes focus. If the eyes go up and to the left: he is imagining imagery. If they go up and to the right: they are remembering imagery. If they simply look left, they are imagining a sound. If they look to the right, they are simply remembering one. If they look down and to the left, they are recalling feelings, scents and tastes. If they are looking down and to the right they are focusing on their internal dialogue.

420. If a person is playing with his hands, looking at them but not staring (brow not furrowed) then he doesn't want to talk to whomever he is talking to. If he isn't looking at his hands but is still "fidgeting" with them, then he is simply thinking intensely. If all his attention is devoted to his hands, he likely has some discomfort in his hands.

421. A person is more likely to be genuinely listening to you if his eyes are roaming about your face, or even watching hand gestures, and not staring into your eyes or at one feature the entire time.

422. If you're trying to get information out of someone, guess at the truth: people attempt to correct what they don't believe to be true.

423. When talking to someone on a phone, a cell phone will have a more "echoing" quality while a landline will have a more "solid" quality.

424. People trying not to cry tend to look up in an attempt to keep back tears.

425. People who would love to prove a point just to be perceived as smart will often use big words and unlikely adjectives in their explanation. People who know a topic well tend to use more simplistic words. A person's uncertainty or defensiveness shows through by his selecting big words to buy time to think about his explanation.

426. When someone is on the phone, it is simple to discern who is on the other line. For instance, if the call is answered in a "laid back" way (For example, "Oh, hi") it is more likely to be a close friend or family member. Anything more refined ("Hello this is [name]") suggests a distant or unknown number.

427. If someone's posture stiffens when on the phone, it is typically an important phone call where he must give his full attention and watch what he says.

428. When someone closes his eyes longer than usual to blink, he is stressed, alarmed or in despair.

429. Someone who is feeling nervous or uncomfortable will automatically try to position himself so that his back is against a wall able to see the whole room.

430. If two people are sitting at a table, you can tell if one is uncomfortable if he tries to place objects in front of himself. He is are trying to distract others from himself.

431. When people are crying silently, they don't want to talk about it: crying aloud indicates a need for attention.

432. As people get more excited they tend to walk faster, and their stride tends to grow longer, because they anticipate something good and want to get to it quickly.

433. To distinguish romantic couples from friends, note the distance apart they are and what they are doing with their hands; hands in pocket/arms folded suggests detachment.

434. If someone pulls at the waist or bottom of his shirt, he may be uncomfortable about his weight or appearance.

435. If someone pulls at the shoulder, neck or back of his shirt, the shirt is probably uncomfortable.

436. If a person suddenly blinks rapidly (especially during conversation) it means he has just had a significant realisation.

437. Someone trying to appear confident when uncomfortable may adopt a stiff and upright posture, which locks the shoulders and keeps the feet squarely apart.

438. People who make frequent references to a specific material are likely to have a large personal interest in the topic, possibly to the point of obsession. It is often a topic they use to fall back on when they don't know what else to talk about.

439. When surrounded by others, people will generally cough or sneeze away from the person they find the most important.

440. People tend to have a different "online voice" which is more confident than their usual "offline" persona.

441. If a person is looking down at reading material, but his eyes are not moving, it suggests that he may be listening to what's going on around them instead of reading.

442. Creating a fictional scenario can tell a lot about people. For example, if someone has chooses to be a character very different from himself, it can be indicator of low self-esteem or desire for change.

443. The simplest way of deducing whether a person likes you is by the expression on his best friend's face.

444. Anonymity often provokes greater aggression in people since the lack of consequences often removes inhibition. (A little like alcohol.)

445. Friends who don't know each other's last names are unlikely to be friends on Facebook or other social network sites that require full names.

446. Someone who is uncharacteristically sentimental with farewells may have lost a loved one in an abrupt manner, such as an accident or heart attack.

447. Some who is thinking about his weight is likely to cross his arms around his middle, to conceal any more evident fat.

448. If someone, when asked, says his favourite artist is Shakespeare or Mozart after hesitation, he cares about how cultured he appears.

449. If someone's typing closely resembles his face-to-face conversations (in tone, commonly used phrases

etc.), it is likely he spends an above average amount of time communicating via a computer.

450. A person who places his bag on his lap immediately after sitting down is often doing so to conceal more of his body: a sign of self-consciousness or worry.

More Codes

The Caesar Cipher is a form of code breaking which requires the use of the following wheel. Both the inner and outer circle rotate to create one of twenty six different codes. The codes work with the inner circle being the letter written and the outer letter being the letter meant. The ciphers are described like the "B cipher" where A would be written as B. The picture below shows the "T cipher" and the codes below are written based on that.

Examples:

SOS: LHL
Hurry: ANKKR
Murder: FNKWXK
Stop: LMHI
Baker Street: UTDXK LMKXXM

Vigenère Cipher:

This is very similar to the Caesar Cipher, but the code changes for each letter. There is a key word which is used to determine the cipher for each letter in the encrypted text. The table below shows the codes if the key word was "deduction." The top row shows the letter meant, with the columns showing the corresponding written letter. For each new letter, you move down a row. If you reach the end of the rows, you go back to the first letter of the code word and continue. The examples given also use the key word of "deduction".

Examples:

SOS: VSV
Hurry: KYULA
Murder: PYUXGK
Stop: VXRJ
Baker Street: EENYT LBFRHX

N	O	I	T	C	U	D	E	D	A
O	P	J	U	D	V	E	F	E	B
P	Q	K	V	E	W	F	G	F	C
Q	R	L	W	F	X	G	H	G	D
R	S	M	X	G	Y	H	I	H	E
S	T	N	Y	H	Z	I	J	I	F
T	U	O	Z	I	A	J	K	J	G
U	V	P	A	J	B	K	L	K	H
V	W	Q	B	K	C	L	M	L	I
W	X	R	C	L	D	M	N	M	J
X	Y	S	D	M	E	N	O	N	K
Y	Z	T	E	N	F	O	P	O	L
Z	A	U	F	O	G	P	Q	P	M
A	B	V	G	P	H	Q	R	Q	N
B	C	W	H	Q	I	R	S	R	O
C	D	X	I	R	J	S	T	S	P
D	E	Y	J	S	K	T	U	T	Q
E	F	Z	K	T	L	U	V	U	R
F	G	A	L	U	M	V	W	V	S
G	H	B	M	V	N	W	X	W	T
H	I	C	N	W	O	X	Y	X	U
I	J	D	O	X	P	Y	Z	Y	V
J	K	E	P	Y	Q	Z	A	Z	W
K	L	F	Q	Z	R	A	B	A	X
L	M	G	R	A	S	B	C	B	Y
M	N	H	S	B	T	C	D	C	Z

Habit

Habits find a way of festering within the lives of any human being. Whether the vice lies with biting nails, with smoking or with sketching, they affect us all. They show areas of weakness, of need for improvement, no matter how trivial. A splintered nail or spattering of ash may be all it takes to break an alibi to pieces.

SH

451. Yellowing of the teeth and between the middle and index finger indicates a person is a frequent smoker.

452. Yellow nails are not always a sign on smoking: they can become discoloured if a proper base coat has not be used before applying coloured nail polish.

453. If a ring is dirty on the outside and clean on the inside it is removed regularly, cleaned by being worked off of the finger.

454. A reason that a ring may be removed frequently is that it risks being submerged in water often, such as through swimming or it may be removed to wash the hands thoroughly.

455. One can determine whether someone always uses a pen by giving him a pencil with which to write. Pen-users will automatically scratch out mistakes rather than erase them, while pencil uses will flip over a pen before realising there is no eraser.

456. A person who usually types will not have a signature so when asked to write one, the signature will either be overly flamboyant or printed.

457. Women who wear high heels frequently have smaller strides than those who don't.

458. A person who often wears high heels will slouch forward noticeably when wearing shoes with a flat sole.

459. Someone who regularly wears heels will walk toe-heel.

460. Someone who wears flat shoes often or walks barefoot will step heel-toe.

461. People who usually wear glasses have marks on the sides of the nose's bridge, left there by the "nose pads".

462. People who recently started wearing new jewellery usually adjust or "fiddle with" it regularly. The same movements are often made in lieu of missing

jewellery. For example, if someone recently lost a necklace she is likely to touch their neck often.

463. Nail biting can be an indication of low self-esteem or anxiety.

464. Generally, if somebody started wearing their glasses only recently, they keep adjusting them; somebody who started wearing glasses a long time ago doesn't bother doing that anymore.

465. A person who keeps touching his nasal bridge or temples when he is trying to focus his eyes usually wears glasses and is unconsciously trying to improve his glasses' position to see better.

466. When someone bites his lip, it can be a sign of arousal, nervousness, or an absent-minded habit, depending on the frequency it is done.

467. Small, vertical lines along the mouth of an older person and yellow stained skin suggest an old smoking habit.

468. A smoker will usually have a smooth patch of skin on the lower lip, usually off to the side.

469. A smoker who is giving up smoking is more likely to have all the signs of having smoked recently, in combination with attempts to hide replacements such as nicotine patches or gum.

470. If someone has callouses on the outside of his thumb, he is a heavy smoker who has not removed the safety from his lighter.

471. People giving up smoking often pick up habits of chewing pens or playing with objects in a similar shape, size and weight to cigarettes to fight off their cravings.

472. If someone wears a piece of jewellery which does not fit or does not match his outfit, it likely holds sentimental value.

473. Someone who smells of smoke but has no sign of smoking habits spends much of their time around those who do smoke.

474. If someone has longer nails on one hand and uneven short ones on the other, it could indicate that he chews his nails on one hand while the other is occupied with an activity. (For example, writing, using a mouse.)

475. If a person has very short painted nails, she is trying to stop biting her nails though more drastic measures.

476. If a person's nails are of average length but are unevenly shaped, it indicates he used to bite his nails but stopped.

477. If a person is accustomed to using a Macintosh computer, he will incorrectly use the key closest to the space bar for key commands on a Windows machine.

478. If he is accustomed to a Windows machine, he will incorrectly use the key farthest from the space bar when using a Mac computer.

479. You can tell which side of his face a person has been sleeping on due to very subtle wrinkles on the side of the face which touches the pillow. (Note you must have good visual reference to notice this difference.)

480. A confident person or someone who enjoys attention tends to swing his hands in a large arc when walking, whereas a more self-conscious or shy person keeps his arms closer to his body.

481. If someone's hair is down and she is wearing a hairband around her wrist, it usually means she prefers to have her hair up, usually around the house or during bad weather conditions.

482. If a person has bitten-down nails; being bitten down to the cuticle or having bitten skin around the nail, the habit is a constant, rather than induced only at times of stress.

483. If a person's shoe is more worn on the outer part of the heel, he walks with his toes pointed slightly outwards.

484. A pigeon-toed person's shoes are more likely to be worn on the inner part of the heel.

485. If nail polish is removed from the bottom up, it usually means that the person wearing the nail polish has picked it off.

486. Nail polish that is removed from the top down usually means it was taken off by accident/blunt force.

487. Someone who wears earphones with the wire going around the top and back of their ear often wears it like that to hide the wire, so you can assume they listen to their mp3 player when they shouldn't, such as in school.

488. People may also wear their earphones with wire going around the top and back of their ear if they wear it while moving a lot, since it makes it harder for the earphone to fall out.

489. If a single finger has a callous in indicates the person is an avid knitter.

490. If a callous has started to peel, whatever activity that causes the callous has not been taking place for several days.

491. A cluster of tiny scratches on new and otherwise flawless jewellery indicates the owner has tried to polish a flaw off himself, either because it needed fixing quickly or he cannot afford to have it professionally cleaned.

492. If there is a slightly "shiny" spot near the base of a person's finger without any other discolouration, that person likely very recently received a ring but wears it constantly: hence the lack of tan line but the beginning of metal discolouration.

493. If someone often sits on his hands, it may be a sign that he has cold hands frequently, meaning he has poor circulation.

494. Usually when a person has a lot of hang nails, he is trying to break the habit of biting his nails.

495. If someone has a callous in the centre of his hand, he may play video games which require him to spin an analogue stick rapidly in full circles; this has been known to cause blisters.

496. A nail-biter of habit will often hide it, as it is something he is trying to stop doing.

497. A nail-biter, due to nervousness, will not make attempts to hide his nail biting since he is preoccupied.

498. If someone smooth's his hands over the backs of her thighs, sweeping from their buttocks to knees, she wears a dress/skirt frequently: this motion stops the clothing from bunching up and wrinkling.

499. The most commonly used computer passwords are "123456," "password," "qwerty" and "abc123".

500. Dry hair, cracked lips, glassy eyes and puffy skin may be a sign one has been drinking heavily for ten or more years, but does not indicate alcoholism or sustained alcohol abuse.

Poisons, Venoms and Toxins

Poison is an underhanded weapon, one which any detective worth his salt must learn to identify and counteract. It is important to consider the distinct differences between poisons, venoms and toxins. Most importantly, he must know how to treat poisoning should he ever need to.

SH

A poison is something that has a noxious effect on living creatures. A toxin is a type of poison which is produced by a living organism. A venom is a toxin injected (not ingested or inhaled) from a living organism into another. A venom is also defined as a toxin and a toxin is defined as a poison. This does not mean all poisons are toxins or that all toxins are venoms.

Aconitum

TITLES:
Aconitum, aconite, monkshood, wolf's bane, leopard's bane, mousebane, women's bane, devil's helmet, queen of poisons, blue rocket.

APPEARANCE:
A tall stem with clusters of large purple, blue, white, pink or yellow flowers. The upper petals are large, and there is a hollow spur at their apex which

contains nectar.

SYMPTOMS:
While in larger doses death is instant, death usually occurs between two and six hours in a fatal poisoning. Early symptoms begin in the stomach, including vomiting, nausea and diarrhoea. Following this, there is burning, tingling and numbness in several areas, including the mouth, face and abdomen. In severe cases, motor weakness and the sensations of tingling and numbness spread to the limbs. Cardiovascular features include hypotension (low blood pressure), ventricular arrhythmias (abnormal heart rhythms from the ventricles) and sinus bradycardia (a sinus node rhythm that is lower than normal). Other symptoms may include dizziness, sweating, headache, confusion, and difficulty in breathing. The main causes of death are connected to the heart: typically from ventricular arrhythmias or paralysis of the heart or respiratory centre. Post mortem, the only signs resemble asphyxia (the body being deprived of oxygen).

TREATMENT:
For aconitum poisoning, gastrointestinal decontamination with activated charcoal may work if given within an hour of consuming the aconitum. Any patients would need to receive monitoring of their blood pressure and cardiac rhythm. The cardiovascular issues may be treated with atropine, lidocaine, amiodarone, bretylium, flecainide, procainamide, and mexiletine. A bypass may be

done along with these medications to help the patient's condition.

Arsenic

TITLES:
Arsenic, Arsenic Trichloride, Arsenic Pentoxide.

APPEARANCE:
Arsenic is a chemical element that is a metalloid, most commonly appearing as metallic grey, yellow and black arsenic allotropes. Grey arsenic is both the most common and the type used in most industrial uses of arsenic. Arsenic is used in pesticides, herbicides, insecticides and treated wood products, though its use is declining.

SYMPTOMS:
Early symptoms of arsenic poisoning are headaches, confusion, drowsiness and severe diarrhoea. Later symptoms are convulsions, and changes in the pigmentation of fingernails may occur. As poisoning becomes acute, the symptoms include vomiting, vomiting blood, blood in urine, hair loss, stomach pain and convulsions. Arsenic poisoning culminates in coma and eventual death.

TREATMENT:
The use of chelating agents dimercaprol and dimercaptosuccinic acid sequester the arsenic away from blood proteins and may help with acute arsenic poisoning. Most treatment focuses on the issues of

hypertension, using treatments designed to treat that ailment.

Asbestos

TITLES:
Asbestos, chrysotile, crocifolite, amosite, anthophyllite, tremolite, actinolite.

APPEARANCE:
Asbestos is a whitish material that was commonly used in buildings for insulation, flooring and roofing but has now been phased out of use. If undisturbed, asbestos doesn't pose a risk. It is dangerous to inhale asbestos fibres, which are released as fine dust when it is damaged.

SYMPTOMS:
Asbestosis is the result of breathing in asbestos fibres over an extended period, resulting in scarring of the lungs. This results in shortness of breath, a persistent cough, wheezing, fatigue, pain in the chest or shoulders and in more advanced cases, clubbed (swollen) fingertips. The complications of scarring in the lungs eventually result in an increased likelihood of lung cancer.

TREATMENT:
Asbestosis can't be cured because its effect is to create irreversible damage to the lungs. There are treatments which can help with this damage such as pulmonary rehabilitation and oxygen therapy, where the patient breathes in oxygen-rich air from a

machine to help improve breathlessness in cases where they have low blood oxygen levels.

Belladonna

TITLES: Atropa belladonna, belladonna, deadly nightshade, devil's cherries, devil's herb, divale, dwale, dwayberry, great morel, naughty man's cherries, poison black cherry.

APPEARANCE: Belladonna plants can be identified by its purple bell-shaped, flowers and cherry-sized green berries that mature to a dark purple or black color. The plant can grow to a height of at least five feet. The plant is native to Europe, North Africa, and Asia. It has been introduced to several other places, such as Ireland and the United States where it can be found growing wild.

SYMPTOMS:
The symptoms of belladonna poisoning can vary greatly. The eyes often exhibit dilated pupils, sensitivity to light and blurred vision. There are also issues with tachycardia, loss of balance and staggering as a result of this. Minor symptoms are headache, rash, flushing, severely dry mouth and throat as well as slurred speech. More severe symptoms include urinary retention, constipation, confusion, hallucinations, delirium, and convulsions.

TREATMENT:
The antidote for belladonna poisoning is physostigmine or pilocarpine, the same as for atropine.

Botulinum

TITLES:
Botulinum toxin A, Botox, Dysport, Xeomin.

APPEARANCE:
The Botulinum toxin is a neurotoxic protein, used for cosmetic botox treatments. It is also used to treat disorders that have symptoms of overactive muscle movement, such as spasms.

SYMPTOMS:
Symptoms are typically localised paralysis, muscle weakness and trouble swallowing, as well headaches and flu like treatments. There may also be issues with blurred or double vision, slurred speech and dry mouth.

TREATMENT:
Treatment is usually limited to an introduction of an antitoxin as soon as possible. While this may help to stop the toxin from doing further damage, it will not "undo" damage that has already been done.

Cyanide

TITLES:

There are many different kinds of cyanide, as cyanide is a chemical compound which contains a carbon triple-bonded to a nitrogen atom.

APPEARANCE:
Cyanide has many different forms, commonly being encountered from breathing in smoke from house fires, metal polishing, insecticides and some seeds such as apricots and apples. Liquid cyanide can also poison an individual by being absorbed through the skin.

SYMPTOMS:
Early symptoms of cyanide poisoning include dizziness, shortness of breath, headache, fast heart rate and vomiting. Later symptoms include slow heart rate, low blood pressure, seizures, unconsciousness and cardiac arrest. These symptoms typically show up within minutes of each other, and should a person survive cyanide poisoning, he may experience neurological problems in the long term.

TREATMENT:
Treatment varies depending on the type of cyanide that an individual has been exposed to. For example, hydrogen cyanide gas only requires decontamination that consists of removing outer clothing and washing hair, while liquids or powders require full decontamination. Treatment will consist of giving the patient 100% oxygen and providing care for the specific symptoms.

Formaldehyde

TITLES:
Formaldehyde, formalin, formic aldehyde, methanediol. Methanol, methyl aldehyde, methylene glycol, methylene oxide.

APPEARANCE:
As a gas formaldehyde is colourless and has a distinct irritating and pungent odour. When condensation happens, the gas converts to several forms of formaldehyde with different chemical formulas. When dissolved in water, it forms methanediol. Formaldehyde is often used in pressed wood products, insulation materials, adhesives and embalming fluid.

SYMPTOMS:

The symptoms of poisoning by formaldehyde vary greatly from case to case. It may cause headaches, skin irritation, eye irritation and breathing problems. If swallowed, formaldehyde can cause burns to oesophagus and stomach. In cases of severe poisoning, symptoms can include restlessness, irregular breathing and heart rhythm, low blood pressure and becoming comatose.

TREATMENT:

Formaldehyde is more complicated than many simple carbon compounds in that it adopts several different forms. As a gas, formaldehyde is colourless and has a characteristic pungent, irritating odour. Upon condensation, the gas converts to various other forms of formaldehyde (with different chemical formulas) that are of more practical value. When dissolved in water, formaldehyde also forms a hydrate, methanediol, with the formula $H_2C(OH)_2$. This compound also exists in equilibrium with various oligomers (short polymers), depending on the concentration and temperature

At concentrations above 0.1 ppm in air formaldehyde can irritate the eyes and mucous membranes, resulting in watery eyes.[43] Formaldehyde inhaled at this concentration may cause headaches, a burning sensation in the throat, and difficulty breathing, and can trigger or aggravate asthma symptoms.

For most people, irritation from formaldehyde is temporary and reversible, though formaldehyde can cause allergies and is part of the standard patch test series

Hemlock

TITLES:
Hemlock, conium maculatum, poison hemlock, Australian carrot fern, Irish devil's bread, poison parsley, spotted corobane, spotted hemlock.

APPEARANCE:

Hemlock grows between five and eight feet tall, with a smooth hollow stem, usually spotted with red or purple on the stem's lower half. The plant is hairless, with small white clustered flowers. The leaves and roots emit an unpleasant odour when crushed.

SYMPTOMS:
This poison is extremely potent, with very small doses leading to respiratory collapse. An adult may die from eating 0.1 gram of the plant. Hemlock poisoning results in muscular paralysis all over the body, ending with paralysis of respiratory systems resulting in a lack of oxygen to the heart and brain.

TREATMENT:
Artificial ventilation to prevent respiratory collapse until the effects have worn off is the most common treatment for hemlock poisoning, usually in place for about 48-72 hours after the poisoning takes place.

Lead

TITLES:
Lead.

APPEARANCE:
Lead is a metallic gray metal that is soft and malleable. When exposed to air, it tarnishes to a dull grey colour. When freshly cut, it has a pale blue tint. Lead is most commonly used in petrol, paint and pipes, although its poisonous properties means its

use is now limited.

SYMPTOMS:
Lead poisoning may lead to headaches, irritability, memory problems, abdominal pain, infertility, tingling in the hands and feet and constipation. It can cause intellectual disability disabilities and behavioural problems. In severe cases, anemia, coma, seizures or death may happen.

TREATMENT:
Treatment for lead poisoning usually involves the use of chelation therapy, which is the infusion of substances intended to remove calcium from the arteries.

Mercury

TITLES:
Mercury, hydrargyrum, liquid silver, quicksilver.

APPEARANCE:
Mercury is a heavy silvery liquid at standard temperatures. It is used in thermometers, barometers, float valves, fluorescent lamps and amalgam based dental fillings though its toxicity means it use is being minimised. Mercury exposure may also happen through eating fish, with fish higher in the food chain more likely to contain dangerous levels.

See also: **Dimethylmercury**

Dimethylmercury is an organomercury compound. It is an incredibly strong neurotoxin that appears as a colourless liquid. While inhaling the vapour enough to be able to smell it would be harmful, it supposedly has a slightly sweet smell, although inhaling enough vapor to detect its odour would be hazardous. Doses as low as 0.1 millilitres can result in severe mercury poisoning, because of the high vapour pressure of the liquid.

SYMPTOMS:
Mercury poisoning can result in itching, burning, pain or even the feeling of insects crawling on or under the skin, skin discolouration (pink fingertips, toes and cheeks), swelling, and shedding skin. Other symptoms may be profuse sweating, increased salivation, high blood pressure and tachycardia (high heart rate). Children may show red cheeks, nose and lips, rashes, muscle weakness, sensitivity to light and loss of hair, teeth and nails. Less common symptoms include kidney dysfunction, memory impairment and insomnia.

TREATMENT:
The treatment of mercury poisoning involves care of the damage the symptoms create and chelation therapy, which is the infusion of substances intended to remove calcium from arteries.

Mustard Gas

TITLES:

Mustard gas, sulfur mustard, blister agent, lewisite, nitrogen mustard, chlorine gas, phosgene oxime.

APPEARANCE:
At room temperature, pure sulfur mustards are colourlesss liquids. When used in an impure form, as they are in warfare, they are usually yellow-brown and have a smell resembling mustard plants, horseradish or garlic.

SYMPTOMS:
It's rare that people exposed to mustard gas show immediate symptoms, which means victims can unknowingly receive high does. Within a day, victims experience intense skin irritation, which eventually turn into large blisters filled with yellow liquid: these are chemical burns. The vapour can easily penetrate clothing, which means the entire body is at risk. If the eyes are affected, they can develop conjunctivitis, and have the eyelids swell, resulting in temporary blindness. In severe cases, the corneas may be damaged in a more permanent way. At extremely high concentrations, mustard agent causes bleeding and blistering within the respiratory system which can result in the system failing. Mustard agent burns are fatal if more than 50% of the body is burned.

TREATMENT:
In less severe mustard agent burns, rehabilitation and skin grafts are often used in order to facilitate recovery.

Ricin

TITLES:
Ricin, ricine, ricins.

APPEARANCE:
Ricin looks like a white powder when prepared as a biotoxin. It is a protein derived from the seeds of the castor bean plant, and can contaminate air, water and food. It is extremely poisonous if injected, injected or inhaled. Purified ricin powder is so powerful, that a dose the size of a few grains of table salt can kill an adult.

SYMPTOMS:
If ingested, ricin can cause pain, haemorrhage and inflammation within the membranes of the gastrointestinal system. This can lead to diarrhoea, nausea, vomiting, difficulty swallowing and bloody vomit or faeces. The low blood volume from the haemorrhage can lead to organ failure in the kidney, liver and pancreas, progressing to shock. Shock and organ failure have symptoms of weakness, drowsiness, disorientation, extreme thirst, low urine production and bloody urine. Early symptoms of ricin inhalation differ, starting with symptoms that include a fever and a cough. When skin or inhalation exposure happens, it can make an allergy develop. Signs of this are asthma, sore, dry throat, congestion, redness of skin, wheezing, itchy and watery eyes, chest tightness and skin irritation.

TREATMENT:

There is no treatment for the poison itself, with treatments instead focusing on the alleviating the various symptoms of ricin poisoning.

Strychnine

TITLES:
Strychnine, Strychnin.

APPEARANCE:
Strychnine is a colourless, bitter alkaloid used as a pesticide to kill birds and rodents. When inhaled, swallowed or absorbed through the eyes, strychnine is highly toxic.

SYMPTOMS:
Poisoning from strychnine results in muscular convulsions and asphyxia.

TREATMENT:
Strychnine poisoning needs early control of muscle spasms, intubation in cases of loss of airway control, decontamination and intravenous hydration.

Tetanospasmin (Tetanus)

TITLES:
Tetanospasmin, tetanus, lockjaw.

APPEARANCE:
Tetanus is caused by an infection with the bacterium Clostridium tetani. This is commonly found in soil,

saliva, manure, and dust. Infection generally occurs due to a break in the skin by a contaminated object.

SYMPTOMS:
Tetanus is characterised by muscle spasms, which most frequently begin in the jaw (hence the name lockjaw) before progressing to the rest of the body. These spasms can last several minutes and can be severe enough to cause bone fractures. Other symptoms include headaches, sweating, fever, high blood pressure, fast heart rate and trouble swallowing. Less well reported symptoms are drooling, excessive sweating, irritability, breathing problems and uncontrolled defecation or urination. Symptoms may set in between three and twenty one days after infection, and may take months to recover from.

TREATMENT:
There is a tetanus antitoxin which is given as an injection. More severe cases require additional steps be taken to be sure that muscle spasms aren't as much of risk, such as tracheotomies which secure the airway. Muscle relaxants may also be prescribed.

Tetrodotoxin

TITLES:
Tetrodoxin, "pufferfish poison".

APPEARANCE:

Tetrodoxin is a neurotoxin carried by an order of species that includes pufferfish, porcupine fish, ocean sunfish and triggerfish. It is produced by infecting or symbiotic bacteria. It can poison a person by ingestion, injection, inhalation or through damaged skin. The poison is found in the liver of certain pufferfish, which must prepared expertly when served to prevent the liver poisoning the rest of the meat.

SYMPTOMS:
The speed with which symptoms appears can vary between 30 minutes and 4 hours, though it has been recorded that fatal doses lead to symptoms within 17 minutes. Tingling of the lips and tongue spreads to the extremities, accompanied by drooling, sweating, weakness, lethargy, headache poor coordination, tremors, paralysis and seizures. Gastrointestinal symptoms include diarrhoea, abdominal pain, nausea and vomiting. The victim may also develop cardiac arrhythmia and paralysis. Some who do not die from tetrodoxin poisoning instead enter a coma.

TREATMENT:
Treatment of tetrodoxin poisoning is non-specific, usually relying on emptying the stomach, trying to bind the toxin by giving the victim activated charcoal and treating individual symptoms.

Common Chemistry

It is quite necessary for any detective hoping to rise in the ranks of police work to have a basic understand of the chemistry that surrounds his daily life. Knowing the makeup of even the most mundane things can be the difference between solving a case and remaining in obscurity.

SH

Acids

A list of common acids from strongest to weakest:
Hydrochloric acid
Sulfuric Acid
Nitric Acid
Phosphoric Acid
Hydrochloric Acid
Ethanoic Acid
Carbonic Acid

Acids react with water when they're added to it, creating ions. The level at which they do this is determines how strong or weak an acid is. Strong acids are more ionised than weak ones.

Concentration is different from strength. Concentration the amount of acid in a solution. A concentrated acid means there is a lot of acid in the volume, while a diluted solution only has a small amount. The pH scale measures the amount of hydrogen ions in a given solution.

The acid dissocation constant K_a is a measure of the strength of an acid. The higher the value of K_a the stronger the acid is. pK_a converts K_a number into a scale that makes it easier to compare the strengths of acids.

	K_a	pK_a
Extremely weak acid	$<10^{-15}$	>15
Very weak acid	$10^{-15}-10^{-5}$	5-15
Weak acid	$10^{-5}-10^{-3}$	3-5
Strong acid	$10^{-3}-0.1$	1-3
Extremely strong acid	>0.1	<1

Beer

Beer is made using the following process, though some may be made with different combinations as there are hundreds of variations on beer.
Milling: this is where dried barley is added and ground down.
Mashing: water is added to produce mort.
Brewing: hops are added and the mixture is boiled
Cooling: the mixture is cooled to somewhere between ten and twenty degrees Celsius.
Fermenting: yeast is added to the mixture, creating alcohol.
Maturing: the mixture is left to mature/
Bottling: the mixture is filtered and then put into bottles.

Alpha Acids
These are in the hops that are used for brewing,
when then degrade and form iso-alpha acids, which
contribute to bitterness. There are many alpha acids,
but some of main ones are prehumulone,
posthumulone, adhumulone, cohumulone and
humulone. Most hops have humulone as their
primary alpha acid.

Beta Acids
These also come from hops and add bitterness
during the fermentation of beer as they're oxidised.
They typically have a harsher bitterness than alpha
acids. The ratio of alpha to beta acids varies
between hops, creating variations between different
beers.

Esters
Esters are formed from the reaction of organic acids,
alcohol in beer and acetyl coenzyme from the hops.
They add fruity flavours to beers. Different types of
beer use different levels of esters; their production is
controlled in many ways, such as fermentation
temperature and the type of yeast that's used.

Essential Oils
These are what give most of hop flavours and
aromas. They are volatile, so are usually gained by
adding hops quite late in the brewing stage. The
three key oils are caryophyllene, humulene and
myrcene. However there are 22 that are known to

give aroma and flavour and over 250 in hops
generally.

Blood

Blood Colour
Haemoglobin is a protein built of smaller sub-units
containing "haems" These contain iron, and it's
their structure that gives oxygenated blood the red
colour. Deoxygenated blood is blue. Gradual blood
loss results in brown blood, as the haemoglobin
oxidises to methaemoglobin.

Blood Types
Blood type is dependent on the presence of certain
antigens. Antigens are on red blood cell surface:
they can bind to antibodies and stimulate immune
responses. The antibodies a blood type has
determine what blood can be received from
transfusions. For example, blood containing A
antigens can't be given to someone with blood that
has A antibodies. O type blood can be given
universally, as it contains no A or B antigens.
Positive blood types have a "rhesus" factor, while
negative blood types do not.

Blood types, listed from most common to least
common.

O+ has A and B antibodies.
A+ has A antigens and B antibodies.
B+ has B antigens and A antibodies.

AB+ has A and B antigens.
O- has A and B antibodies.
A- has A antigens and B antibodies.
B- has B antigens and A antibodies.
AB- had A and B antigens.

The Smell of Blood

The metallic smell of blood is given by the compound *trans*-4,5-epoxy-2-decenal. The smell of metals and blood interacting is due to oct-1-en-3-one, produced due to the reaction of the iron in haemoglobin with oxidised skin lipids.

Bodily Fluids

Bile
Bile is coloured by to two different pigments. The green is due to bilverdin, which is haem from damaged red cells that has been converted. This bilverdin is converted into a brown pigment called bilirubin. Both of these also cause the colouring around bruises.

Faeces
Stercobilin is from bilirubin being broken down by microbes in the intestines, which is then broken down further into stercobilin. Stercobilin is responsible for the brown colour of faeces.

Urine

Bilirubin is broken down into urobilinogen by the microbes in the intestines. This can then be absorbed into the bloodstream, and oxidised to create urobilin. Urobilin is secreted from the kidneys and gives urine its yellow colour. Clearer urine is typically from diluting urobilin with water.

Chocolate

Cocoa solids are what remain after cocoa butter is extracted from cacao beans. These contain phenethylamine which makes people feel good. Cocoa solids also contain theobromine which is toxic to dogs. American chocolate is often slightly sour due to the inclusion of butyric acid. Types of chocolate differ due to the level of cocoa solids in them.

Dark Chocolate

Dark chocolate has more than 35% cocoa solids. The average lethal dose of dark chocolate for dogs is 300mg per kg of the dog's body weight.

Milk Chocolate

Milk chocolate contains 20 to 30% cocoa solids. Some chocolate makers add vanillin to milk chocolates to enhance their taste.

White Chocolate

White chocolate contains zero cocoa solids, instead containing cocoa butter, sugar and milk. Cocoa butter is made of several fats, primarily palmitic acid and stearic acid.

Coloured LED lights

LEDs are light-emitting diodes, which illuminate when a current goes through the semiconducting materials within them. The colour of the light is dependent upon the materials within the LED.

Red lights contain gallium arsenide phosphide (GaAsP) and aluminium gallium indium phosphide (AlGaInP).

Yellow lights contain gallium arsenide phosphide (GaAsP) and aluminium gallium indium phosphide (AlGaInP) in different concentrations than red lights.

Green lights contain gallium phosphide (GaP) and gallium nitride (GaN).

Blue lights contain indium gallium nitrate (InGaN) and aluminium gallium nitride (AlGaN).

Fingerprint detection

Types of Fingerprint

Latent Prints:

These prints are made by the body's natural sweat and oils. They remain on hard surfaces and are only made visible by the use of various techniques. Sometimes to expose hidden fingeprints, surfaces are exposed to cyanoacrylate fumes to make them visible. Cyanoacrylates are used in superglue, and make a white 3D matrix when in contact with fingerprint residue.

Patent Prints:

These prints are visible on hard surfaces, and can be photographed without needing any additional treatment to make them more visible. These techniques rely on the use of powders that usually contain binders (such as rosin, iron powder or gum arabic) and pigments (such as aluminium, copper powders and zinc). The binder makes the powder cling to the moist/oily residue left by fingerprints, and the pigment colours the prints to make them easier to visualise.

Plastic Prints:

These are three-dimensional fingerprints, which are made on soft surfaces like wet paint and wax. Like patent prints, these are visible without needing additional treatment.

Chemical Developers

Some finger print detection involves using chemical developers, which react with the amino acids in sweat to colour fingerprints and improve their visibility. Ninhydrin is used to make them appear purple, while 1,2-diazafluoren-9-one (DFO) makes fingerprints glow in some lights.

Fireworks

Firework colours

Red fireworks contain strontium salts, like strontium nitrate, strontium carbonate and strontium sulfate.

Orange fireworks contain calcium salts, like calcium chloride, calcium carbonate and calcium sulfate.

Yellow fireworks contain sodium salts, like sodium nitrate, cryolite and sodium oxalate.

Green fireworks contain barium salts, like barium nitrate, barium carbonate, barium chloride and barium chlorate.

Blue fireworks contain copper salts, like copper oxide, copper carbonate and copper chloride.

Purple fireworks combine the copper compounds from blue fireworks and the strontium compounds from red fireworks.

Silver fireworks contain aluminium and white-hot magnesium.

White fireworks contain burning metal like magnesium, titanium and aluminium.

Firework Components

Fuel allows the fireworks to burn, with gun powder (a combination of potassium nitrate, charcoal and sulfur) being a common fuel

Oxidisers provide oxygen for the fuel to burn, usually being nitrates, perchlorates or chlorates.

Binders hold the mixture within the firework together, with the most common one being starch and dextrin dampened with water.

Chlorine donors are used to make the colours stronger in fireworks, with some oxidisers helping with the process.

Gemstones

When comparing gemstones, the Mohs scale of mineral hardness is used as a scale characterizing the level of scratch resistance of various minerals.

Alexandrite is coloured by chromium ions replacing aluminium is some places, with its colour varying in certain lights. Their formula is Al_2BeO_4 with a mohs hardness of 8.5.

Amethysts are made purple by the irradiation of iron 3+ ions in place of silicon in some locations in the structure. Their fomula is SiO_2 with a mohs hardness of 7.

Aquamarine is blue due iron 2+/3+ ions replacing aluminium ions in some locations in its structures. Their formula $Be_3Al_2(SiO_3)_6$ with a mohs hardness of 7.5 to 8.

Citrine is made yellow is due to presence of aluminium or iron impurities. Their formula is SiO_2 with a mohs hardness of 7.

Diamonds are colourless, but can be faintly coloured by the trapping of nitrogen or boron atoms in them. Their formula is C_n with a mohs hardness of 10.

Emeralds are green due to chromium ions replacing aluminium in some places in it's structure. Their formula is $Be_3Al_2(SiO_3)_6$ with a mohs hardness of 7.5 to 8.

Garnet is made red by the same process that peridot is made green. Their formula $Mg_3Al_2(SiO_4)_3$ with a mohs hardness of 6.5 to 7.5.

Jades are made green from chromium and iron impurities. The formula is $NaAlSi_2O_6$ with a mohs hardness of 6.5 to 7.

Opals are a mixture of colours due the diffraction of light passing through them. Their formula is $SiO_2.nH_2O$ with a mohs hardness of 5.5 to 6.

Pearls are produced in the soft tissue of shelled mollusks, with thinner layers making the lustre finer. Their formula is $CaCo_3$, with a mohs hardness of 2.5 to 4.5.

Peridot is made green by iron 2+ ions replacing magnesium ions in some locations in its structure. Their formula is Mg_2SiO_4 with a mohs hardness of 6.5 to 7.

Rubies are made red by chromium ions replacing aluminium ions in some places in their structure. Their formula is Al_2O_3 with a mohs hardness of 9.

Sapphires are made blue by titanium and iron ions replacing aluminium ions in some locations in the structure. Their formula Al_2O_3 with a mohs hardness of 9.

Spinel can be a variety of colours due to impurities such as nickel, chromium and iron. The formula is $MgAl_2O_4$ with a mohs hardness of 7.5 to 8.

Topaz is colourless when pure, but can be blue or brown with certain atomic imperfections $Al_2SiO_4(F,OH)_2$ with a mohs hardness of 8.

Tourmaline is pink due to manganese ions replacing aluminium and lithium ions in some places. The formula is $Na_3Li_3Al_6(BO_3)_3(SiO_3)_6F_4$ with a mohs hardness of 7 to 7.5.

Turquoise is made green by the presence of copper ions coordinated to water and hydroxide ions. Their formula is $A_6(PO_4)_4(OH)_8.4H_2O$ with a mohs hardness of 5 to 6.

Zircon can be a large variety of colours depending on the impurities they have, with the colourless variety being a popular diamond substitution. Their formula is $ZrSiO_4$ with a mohs hardness of 7.5.

Matches

Matches differ in composition depending on their type. They will contain an oxidising agent in the matchhead and red phosphorus in the striking surface.
When striking a match, the oxidiser and phosphorus combine and are heated by the friction of striking the match.

In matches, the material in the matchhead varies. Potassium chlorate is the main ingredient in the heads of safety matches.
Phosphorus sesquisulfide is used in the head of strike anywhere matches.
Matches also contain ammonium phosphates to prevent "after glow," glue to bind the materials that make them, and paraffin wax to make them burn more easily.

Nail polish

Nail polish contains a polymer that is dissolved in a solvent, which is called a firm-forming polymer. When nail polish is applied, the solvent evaporates and polymer forms a film.

Gel nail polish is instead of made up of a photoinitiator like benzoyl peroxide and methacrylate monomers. When exposed to UV light, polymerisation and solidification is triggered.

Pigments in nail polish colour are organic (carbon-based) or inorganic (for example, iron oxide). Thermochromic (changes colour depending on temperature) and photochromic (changes colour depending on light level) pigments are also used.

In order to make nail polishes last longer, stabilisers are added to prevent the colour fading from the nail polish from prolonged exposure to sunlight.

Solvents are a vital element to nail polish, with butyl acetate and ethyl acetate being rather common choices of solvent. It is the solvent that creates the characteristic smell of nail polish. Nail polish remover uses ethyl acetate and acetone.

Red Lipstick

Composition

Red lipstick contains:

65% castor oil
15% beeswax
10% miscellaneous waxes
5% lanolin
5% pigments, perfume and dyes.

Waxes

Waxes are what give the lipstick its structure. Some natural waxes that are used are beeswax, candelila wax and carnauba wax. Carnauba wax has the highest melting point of any wax, which makes it a common choice for lipstick to prevent it from melting too easily. Oils give lipstick more lubrication so it's easier to apply, as well as making it glossy. The most commonly used one is castor oil

Ingredients

Lipstick colour is determined the pigments and dyes used in it. Carmine red is derived from scale insects, while eosin is a dye which reacts with amino groups in the skin to create a deep red colour. Titanium dioxide is used to dilute these colours to create pink shades. Fragrances might be added to mask the chemical smells. Some lipsticks include mild skin irritants like capsaicin to induce plumping of the lips.

Roses

Colour

Roses can vary in colour greatly due to the chemical pigments they have. Several cartoenoids like rubixanthin and zeaxanthin make the roses shades of yellow and orange. Anthocyanins like cyanin and pelargonin are what give roses red shades. It's a combinations of these compounds that creates the range of colours seen in roses.

Smell of roses

The smell of roses is due to several chemical compounds. The concentration of these chemical compounds isn't what determines how strong they are. Some key contributors to the rose aroma are nerol, geraniol, citronellol and 2-phenylethanol.

Wine

Composition

On average, wine contains:
86% water
12% ethanol
1% glycerol
0.4% organic acids
0.1% tannins and phenolics
0.5% other compounds

Anthocyanins

Anthocyanins are in the skin in grapes; they react with other chemicals in wine to produce polymeric pigments. Anthocyanins are coloured on their own, but the colour varies depending on the pH.

Flavan-3-Ols

Flavan-3-ols are in the seeds of grapes and are notably bitter. They can be in up to 800 milligrams per litre of wine. 20 milligrams per litre is what is required to produce a bitter taste.

Flavonols

Flavonols can help improve colour of red wine, through "co-pigmentation". These compounds have potential anti-carcinogenic and anti-oxidant effects but rarely have this effect in at a high enough levels in wine to contribute any health benefits.

Tannins

Tannins are polymers of other chemicals in wine. Condensed tannins are polymers of flavan-3-ols and are what cause a dry mouthed feeling after drinking. Changes in tannin over time are what make aging a wine improve

Lock Picking

In the average case, a detective will face hundreds of doors that inhibit forward progress. While lock picking is a not a habit a respectable individual should rely on too often, it is important that a detective understands each tool in his arsenal.

SH

Types of Locks:

Lever tumbler locks

A level tumbler lock is a lock that uses a set of
levers to prevent the bolt from moving in the lock.
Usually the lock is opened by lifting the individual
tumblers above a predetermined height. The number
of levers will vary from lock to lock, but it is most
commonly an odd number of tumblers for a door
which can be opened from either side. This is to
preserve symmetry, allowing for the same key open
the lock on either side. The lock is made up of
levers, usually made out of non-ferrous materials.
Typically, the middle of the levers are cut away to
various depths to create different combinations. A
lever will have pockets or gates that the bolt moves
during locking. Lever locks usually have a bitted
key, with higher security locks like safes using a
double-bitted key. A three lever lock is a common
type of lever lock, but is usually only used for low
security situations like internal doors, as they are
easier to pick. Five lever locks are the recommended
ones to use for general home security. Many
modern lever tumbler locks have anti pick devices,
along with hardened bolts and anti-drill plates to
make them less vulnerable to physical attack.

Pin tumbler locks

A pin tumbler lock or Yale lock is a mechanism that
uses pins of differing lengths to stop the lock from
opening without the right key. Pin tumblers are
most often used in cylinder locks, but can be found

in ace locks. A cylinder lock is an outer casing with a cylindrical hole in which the plug is kept: in order to open the lock, the plug needs to rotate. The plug has a straight-slot, the other end may have a lever, which activates a mechanism to retract the locking bolt. This series of holes, approximately five or six of them, are drilled into the plug, contains key pins of various lengths, which are round to allow the key to slide over them easier. Each of these key pins has a responding set of driver pins above it, which are spring loaded. Locks may have only one driver pin for each key pin, but more complex locks may have extra driver pins called spacer pins. When the plug and outer casing are put together, the pins are pushed down into the plug by the springs. The point where the plug and cylinder meet is the shear point. With a key that fits, the pins will rise, aligning exactly at the shear point. This lets the plug rotate and opens the lock.

Wafer tumbler locks

A cylindrical wafer tumbler lock gas a series of flat wafers that hold a cylindrical plug in place. Wafers are fitted into vertical slots in the plug and are spring-loaded causing them to protrude into opposing wide grooves in the casing of the lock. As long as any wafers protrude into one of the grooves, the plug can't rotate and open. This is what happens if a key that doesn't fit is used in the lock. A rectangular hole is cut into the middle of each wafer: the vertical position of the holes in the wafers varies, so a key needs to have notches corresponding to the height of the hole in each wafer. This is so each wafer is pulled in to point where the wafer edges are flush with the plug and allowing for it rotate and open. Wafer tumbler locks are often used on desk drawers, key switches, electrical panels, cabinets, lockers and cash boxes. Some wafer tumbler locks use a stack of closely spaced wafers designed to fit the contour of a double-sided key. Wafer tumbler locks can use single or double bitted keys.

Lock Picking Keys

Skeleton keys

The skeleton key or warded pick, is used for opening locks without a specifically fitted key. They are made to fit a generalised key shape that is simpler than the actual key, to allow for internal manipulations. A skeleton key is only used to open warded locks, which only need the back end of the lock manipulated to open. Some locks have side grooves in keys to prevent the use of skeleton keys, though thinner skeleton keys can bypass this.

Jigglers or try out keys

Most wafer tumbler locks can be opened with "jigglers" or try-out keys. These are sets of keys which are designed with several of the most common key patterns available. The try out key is inserted like a normal key, while the key is rocked back and forth and turned until the lock opens.

Lock Picking Tools

Curtain pick

Curtain picks can open lever tumbler locks.

Torsion wrench

A torsion wrench is always needed when picking a tumbler or wafer lock, even when you have a pick gun. It's used to apply torque to the plug of a torsion wrench to hold any picked pins in. Once all the pins are picked, the torsion wrench is used to turn the plug and therefore open the lock. The torsion wrench is usually shaped like a letter "L". Other torsion tools, especially those for unlocking cars, resemble tweezers and allow you to apply torque to the top and bottom of the lock.

Half-diamond pick

This pick is in most lock picking kits, and is mainly used for picking individual pins, but can used for wafer and disk locks. The angles that form the base of the half-diamond can be steep or shallow, depending on the need for picking without needing to affect neighbouring pins. A normal lock picking set has approximately three half diamond picks and a full diamond pick.

Hook pick

The hook pick is like a half-diamond pick, instead having a hook-shaped tip rather than a half-diamond shape. The hook pick is considered one of the most basic lock-picking tools and can be the only tool needed by a professional picking a lock not requiring "raking" or a pick gun. Hook picks usually come in a variety of sizes and shapes in a typical lock-picking set.

Ball pick

The ball is pick is like the half-diamond pick, but has a half or full circle shape at its tip. This is often used to open wafer locks.

Rake picks

There are many types of rake picks, designed to rake pins by rapidly sliding the pick past all the pins repeatedly until they reach the height required to unlock them. This method requires less skill and experience than attempting to pick each pin individually, and is usually more effective on cheaper locks. There are also more advanced rake picks available that are designed to mimic different pin heights.

Decoder pick

The decoder pick is a key has been adapted such that the height of it notches can be changed. This is done either by screwing them into the blade base of by adjusting them from the handle while the key is in the lock. It allows access to the lock as well as template for cutting a new key.

Bump keys

A simple way to open most pin locks is to insert a key which has been cut so that each peak of the key is equal and has been cut down to lowest groove of the key. The key is then struck sharply with a hammer while applying torque. The force is carried down the key and will move only the driver pins leaving the key pins in place. When done correctly this creates a gap around the shear line allowing the plug to rotate. Some modern locks with higher security levels include bumping protection.

Pick guns (snap guns)

The manual pick gun or snap gun uses a similar principle to bump keys, transferring energy to key pins to make them jump and allowing the cylinder to turn. The pick gun usually has a trigger that creates this movement, and is a modern staple of lock-picking kits.

Tubular lock pick

A tubular lock pick is a specialised tool specifically for opening a tubular pin tumbler lock. These tubular lock picks are very similar in design and come in a variety of sizes to fit most tubular locks.

The tool is inserted into the lock and turned clockwise with medium torque. As the tool is pushing in, each of the pins is slowly forced down until they stop, binding the driver pins behind the shear line of the lock. Using a pick like this means that locks can be opened in a few seconds. Most tubular lock picks come with a decoder which allows the person using it to know what the depth is required from the pins to unlock the door. By using this decoder it allows a tubular key to be cut.

Index

Acting: Numbers 14, 22, 23, 24, 25, 59, 63.

Appearance: Numbers 13, 27, 29, 42, 45, 46, 52, 53, 54, 56, 61, 62, 65, 69, 70, 81, 97, 98, 99, 100, 103, 111, 114, 118, 119, 120, 127, 129, 131, 135, 137, 138, 141, 160, 164, 174, 175, 176, 194, 198, 199, 206, 216, 220, 249, 250, 255, 259, 268, 269, 273, 276, 279, 285, 286, 287, 290, 291, 292, 293, 294, 296, 300, 302, 303, 304, 307, 320, 321, 326, 327, 328, 341, 343, 359, 360, 364, 372, 373, 384, 384, 387, 472, 479, 481, 483, 484, 491, 499, 500

Artists: Numbers 34, 49, 56, 65, 67, 289, 319, 364, 376.

Band Members: Numbers 141, 146, 158, 161.

Body Language: Numbers 15, 16, 19, 24, 25, 26, 28, 35, 40, 43, 47, 57, 58, 59, 63, 64, 68, 85, 86, 88, 92, 93, 94, 95, 96, 102, 104, 105, 106, 107, 108, 109, 110, 115, 116, 117, 121, 122, 123, 124, 125, 126, 130, 132, 133, 134, 136, 142, 146, 155, 157, 158, 159, 161, 162, 166, 170, 173, 178, 182, 184, 195, 196, 197, 200, 201, 202, 203, 204, 205, 208, 219, 223, 228, 229, 232, 238, 239, 245, 257, 258,

160, 261,266, 267, 272, 278, 288, 301, 305, 308,
309, 312, 313, 314, 315, 316, 322, 323, 324, 325,
329, 339, 331, 332, 333, 334, 335, 336, 337, 338,
339, 340, 342, 344, 345, 345, 348, 349, 350, 351,
352, 353, 354, 355, 356, 358, 371, 374, 378, 385,
388, 389, 391, 397, 398, 399, 400, 402, 403, 404,
412, 413, 414, 415, 416, 418, 419, 420, 421, 424,
428, 429, 431, 432, 433, 434, 435, 436, 437, 439,
441, 442, 443, 447, 450, 451, 457, 458, 459, 460,
461, 462, 464, 465, 466, 467, 468, 469, 471, 475,
476, 477, 478, 480, 485, 486, 493, 498.

Callouses: Numbers 11, 30, 49, 50, 55, 70, 90, 97,
98, 112, 113, 128, 131, 140, 144, 145, 149, 150,
165, 172, 306, 350, 363, 470, 489, 490, 495.

Computers: Numbers 8, 74, 75, 258, 263, 274, 280,
440, 444, 445, 449, 456, 477, 478, 499.

Crime: Numbers 390, 401, 402, 403, 406, 407, 410,
416.

Dance: Numbers 59, 64, 94, 95, 96, 97, 98, 100,
101, 102, 103, 117, 124, 130, 135, 137, 356.

Dirt: Numbers 10, 11, 199, 212, 225, 241, 259, 319,
375, 453.

Feet: Numbers 23, 57, 58, 82, 84, 85, 88, 92, 93, 94, 97, 98, 99, 100, 102, 107, 115, 127, 130, 132, 136, 137, 141, 146, 194, 205, 261, 273, 284, 359, 360, 371, 378, 437, 459, 460, 483, 484.

Guitar: Numbers 151, 152, 153, 154, 164, 165, 303.

Glasses: Numbers 331, 337, 404, 461, 464, 465.

Gymnasts: Numbers 103, 117, 134, 135.

Hair: Numbers 25, 29, 54, 211, 220, 260, 268, 281, 282, 283, 295, 349, 481, 500.

Hands: Numbers 10, 11, 12, 13, 30, 31, 32, 33, 34, 36, 37, 41, 44, 49, 50, 51, 55, 66, 67, 87, 89, 90, 91, 101, 112, 113, 128, 131, 139, 140, 144, 145, 147, 148, 149, 150, 151, 152, 153, 154, 163, 165, 167, 168, 169, 171, 172, 254, 263, 271, 274, 283, 289, 306, 310, 346, 357, 361, 362, 363, 365, 366, 367, 375, 377, 452, 453, 454, 455, 463, 470, 474, 482, 489, 490, 492, 494, 495, 496, 497.

Handwriting: Numbers 60, 71, 72, 73, 76, 77, 78, 79, 80, 186, 187, 188, 189, 190, 191, 317, 318, 456.

Handedness: Numbers 361, 362, 363, 364, 365, 366, 367, 368, 369, 370, 371, 372, 373, 374, 375,

376, 378, 379, 380, 381, 382, 383, 384, 385, 386, 387.

Health: Numbers 322, 323, 324, 325, 326, 327, 328, 329, 330, 331, 332, 333, 334, 335, 336, 337, 338, 339, 340, 341, 342, 343, 344, 345, 346, 347, 348, 349, 350, 351, 352, 353, 354, 355, 356, 357, 358, 359, 360.

Home: Numbers 208, 209, 210, 211, 212, 213, 214, 215, 216, 217, 218, 219, 220, 221, 222, 223, 224, 225, 226, 227, 228, 229, 230, 231, 232, 233, 234, 235, 236, 237, 238, 239, 240, 241, 242, 243, 244, 245, 246, 247, 248, 249, 250, 251, 252.

Interaction: Numbers 414, 415, 416, 417, 418, 419, 420, 421, 422, 423, 424, 425, 426, 427, 428, 429, 430, 431, 432, 433, 434, 435, 436, 437, 438, 439, 440, 441, 442, 443, 444, 445, 446, 447, 448, 449, 450.

Jewellery: Numbers 56, 285, 295, 300, 373, 453, 454, 462, 472, 491, 492.

Lips: Numbers 45, 166, 308, 345, 500.

Lying: Numbers 388, 389, 391, 392, 393, 394, 395, 396, 397, 298, 399, 400, 403, 404, 405, 408, 409, 411, 412, 413, 418.

Medical Profession: Numbers 12, 27, 28, 29, 37, 38, 39, 40, 66, 67, 73, 290, 291.

Music: Numbers 139, 140, 141, 142, 143, 144, 145, 146, 147, 148, 149, 150, 151, 152, 153, 154, 155, 156, 157, 158, 159, 160, 161, 162, 163, 164, 165, 166, 167, 168, 169, 170, 171, 172, 173, 174, 175, 176.

Nail Biting: Numbers 463, 471, 474, 475, 493, 497.

On Person: Numbers 177, 179, 181, 230, 253, 256, 281, 282, 284, 295, 297, 298, 299, 370, 487, 488.

Piano: Numbers 147, 148, 171, 241, 242.

Shoes: Numbers 27, 41, 70, 81, 119, 120, 127, 132, 137, 194, 259, 273, 284, 286, 292, 293, 343, 359, 457, 458, 459, 460, 483, 484.

Singing: Numbers 15, 16, 17, 18, 19, 20, 21, 22, 23, 25, 42, 59, 64.

Skin: Numbers 11, 249, 260, 268, 274, 289, 320, 341, 347, 366, 467, 468, 482, 500.

Smoking: Numbers 63, 64, 322, 451, 468, 469, 473.

Speech: Numbers 14, 17, 18, 20, 38, 39, 48, 156, 192, 193, 207, 217, 218, 221, 224, 247, 248, 264, 265, 270, 275, 277, 329, 392, 393, 394, 395, 396, 401, 405, 406, 407, 408, 409, 412, 417, 422, 423, 425, 426, 427, 431, 438, 440, 444, 445, 446, 448, 449.

Sport: Numbers 81, 82, 83, 84, 85, 86, 87, 88, 89, 90, 91, 92, 93, 94, 95, 96, 97, 98, 99, 100, 101, 102, 103, 104, 105, 106, 107, 108, 109, 110, 111, 112, 113, 114, 115, 116, 117, 118, 119, 120, 121, 122, 123, 124, 125, 126, 127, 128, 129, 130, 131, 132, 133, 134, 135, 136, 137, 138.

String Instruments: Numbers 140, 143, 144, 145, 157, 159, 160, 167, 168, 169, 170, 172, 175, 176.

Surroundings: Numbers 75, 82, 83, 84, 180, 183, 185, 209, 210, 211, 212, 213, 214, 215, 222, 225, 226, 227, 231, 233, 234, 235, 236, 237, 240, 241, 242, 243, 244, 246, 251, 252, 262, 280, 311, 319, 368, 369, 376, 379, 380, 396, 390, 410, 430.

Travel: Numbers 177, 178, 179, 180, 181, 182, 183, 184, 185, 186, 187, 189, 190, 191, 192, 193, 194, 195, 196, 197, 198, 199, 200, 201, 202, 203, 204, 205, 206, 207.

Weight: Numbers 64, 307, 434, 447.

Work: Numbers 10, 11, 12, 13, 14, 15, 16, 17, 18, 19, 20, 21, 22, 23, 24, 25, 26, 27, 28, 29, 30, 31, 32, 33, 34, 35, 36, 37, 38, 39, 40, 41, 42, 43, 44, 45, 46, 47, 48, 49, 50, 51, 52, 53, 54, 55, 56, 57, 58, 59, 60, 61, 62, 63, 64, 65, 66, 67, 68, 69, 70.

Wind Instruments: Numbers 149, 150, 155, 158, 156, 157, 162, 166, 174.

Writing: Numbers 71, 72, 73, 74, 75, 76, 77, 78, 79, 80.

Also from MX Publishing

THE MONOGRAPHS

BEN CARDALL

The Monographs - A comprehensive manual on all you need to know to become an expert Deductionist.

Have you ever wanted to truly know what goes on inside the head of Sherlock Holmes? Have you wanted to be able to read people and their expressions like books? Have you ever wanted to read a room and all the tells and clues that it provides? Then this is the book for you. The Monographs is a complete and comprehensive manual that will impart the lessons on everything you need to know to become a Deductionist in today's world.